Robbie's pulse racing

Had to be from all the caffeine she'd chugged that morning, not the appreciative gleam in Holden's eyes. She licked her lips and managed to reply, "Thank you..."

"I'm the one who should be thanking you."

A giggle slipped out. And she never giggled. "For what? The lecture I gave you this morning?"

"For saving my life the other night."

"You'd probably have gotten hurt less if you'd taken your chances with the bullets."

She lifted her fingertips to his cheek. The scrape had scabbed over, the flesh beneath it bruised, but the injury took nothing away from his devastating good looks. Her fingertips tingled from the contact with his skin. "I'm sorry you got hurt."

"You were right. I had no business being there." He leaned closer. "And I have no business doing this...."

His lips touched hers, as tentatively and gently as she'd touched his cheek.

Dear Reader,

I hope you're enjoying reading the CITIZEN'S POLICE ACADEMY miniseries as much as I'm enjoying writing it. *Once a Cop* was especially fun to write, because it's the heroine who is in law enforcement. Roberta Meyers is such a remarkable woman—a tough single mother who's determined to keep the streets safe for her daughter and the rest of the people of the city of Lakewood, Michigan.

When youth minister Holden Thomas gets caught in the middle of a police raid he falls for Robbie, but Holden's looking for security above all else in a relationship. So the last woman with whom he'd want to get involved is one who is in danger every time she clocks in for a shift. But then his niece and Robbie's daughter decide they want to become sisters instead of just best friends, and there's a matchmaking free-for-all. Will Holden come to accept that Robbie is the right woman for him?

Happy reading!

Lisa Childs

Once a Cop
LISA CHILDS

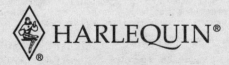

HARLEQUIN®

TORONTO • NEW YORK • LONDON
AMSTERDAM • PARIS • SYDNEY • HAMBURG
STOCKHOLM • ATHENS • TOKYO • MILAN • MADRID
PRAGUE • WARSAW • BUDAPEST • AUCKLAND

Recycling programs
for this product may
not exist in your area.

ISBN-13: 978-0-373-75278-2

ONCE A COP

Copyright © 2009 by Lisa Childs-Theeuwes.

ABOUT THE AUTHOR

Bestselling, award-winning author Lisa Childs writes paranormal and contemporary romance for Harlequin/Silhouette Books. She lives on thirty acres in west Michigan with her husband, two daughters, a talkative Siamese and a long-haired Chihuahua who thinks she's a rottweiler. Lisa loves hearing from readers, who can contact her through her Web site, www.lisachilds.com, or snail mail address, P.O. Box 139, Marne, MI 49435.

Books by Lisa Childs

Don't miss any of our special offers. Write to us at the following address for information on our newest releases.

Harlequin Reader Service
U.S.: 3010 Walden Ave., P.O. Box 1325, Buffalo, NY 14269
Canadian: P.O. Box 609, Fort Erie, Ont. L2A 5X3

To Senior Editor Kathleen Scheibling,
for always helping me make the book better!

Chapter One

The raid is going down soon. Adrenaline coursed through Officer Robbie Meyers's veins, quickening her pulse, as she blinked against the smoke and glanced at the dial of her watch. *Real soon.*

She resisted the urge to reach beneath her zip-up sweatshirt and check for the presence of her gun and cuffs. The weight of the holstered weapon rested against the small of her back, reassuring her that she was ready—for whatever happened. She had to be ready. It wasn't only her fellow officers who were depending on her to do her job well.

She forced a vacant, flirtatious smile onto her face and wiggled her body on the dance floor, which was actually just a section of cracked cement floor in the abandoned warehouse. The warehouse wasn't abandoned tonight, though, since teenagers and twenty-somethings completely filled the space. Music, at a deafening volume, echoed off the walls and the high metal ceiling.

"Rob, do you see him yet?" a voice asked through the small plastic piece in her ear.

She scanned the crowd for the face of the dealer they were hoping to find at tonight's rave. They'd had a tip he was going to be there with a special shipment for the customers gathered at the party.

This could be her biggest bust since joining vice six months ago. Regret tugged at her, though, over what she'd had to miss in order to participate in the raid.

Yet how could she have asked for time off when the Lakewood Police Department was already short-staffed? Despite having several officers called back to active duty in the National Guard, the city council wouldn't approve the chief's request to hire more police.

Nerves unsettled Robbie's empty stomach as she noted flashes of metal at the waists of some of the kids there. She wasn't the only one carrying. This was not a good night to be understaffed.

"Rob, can you hear me?" the voice asked.

"Yeah…"

The kid with whom she was dancing took it as an invitation to reach for her. She stepped back, and with a shake of her head slipped through the gyrating bodies. As she pushed through the crowd, she spotted *him* coming through the open garage doors in the loading-dock area. The department hadn't been able to find a clear picture of the dealer, but this guy fit the general description: about thirty, tall and lean, brown hair. His hair was thick, with sun streaks, and his skin was deeply tanned. The guy probably dealt on the beach, too, as Lakewood was on the Lake Michigan shore. He certainly seemed to know the teens and he moved from one to another talking briefly with them, as if he was looking for someone in particular. Then he lifted his head and his gaze met hers.

He's made me for a cop.

HOLDEN THOMAS searched his mind, as he'd searched the crowd, for any recollection of the black-haired girl who was standing in front of him. He didn't remember seeing her around before, either at his shelter for runaway teenagers, or at the youth center at St. Mike's, where he'd worked before opening up the shelter. She wasn't the girl he'd come here to help tonight, but he suspected she might be in just as much trouble.

Her eyes widened as he met her gaze, and he caught a glimpse of fear in the icy-blue depths. But when he closed the short distance between them she masked the fear with bravado.

"Who are you?" she asked with the familiar belligerence with which teens usually greeted him the first time—and sometimes several times after—they met.

"Someone you can trust," he promised her. These kids had so few people they could rely on.

She laughed, a deep-throated chuckle that had him taking another look at her. Was she really the teenager he'd pegged her for? Or was she older?

She wore the ripped jeans and hoodie that were the current teenage uniform. She had that Goth thing going on, too, with black eyeliner heavily outlining her thick-lashed blue eyes, and her skin was pale, even though summer in west Michigan was only just slipping away as September began. Most of these kids should have school tomorrow, but he doubted that many, if any, would be attending class in the morning. Would she?

"What's your name?" he asked.

But before she could answer, the night erupted with light and noise, louder than the music, which had abruptly cut off. Men in black uniforms and bulletproof vests stormed the warehouse. "Lakewood PD. Stay where you are!"

Then shots rang out, short and earsplitting. He reached to protect the girl as something whizzed near his head. One moment Holden was standing; the next pain exploded in his shins, his legs gave out and he struck the concrete floor. A knee dug into the small of his back and his wrists were wrenched behind him and cuffed.

Silky hair fell across his cheek when she leaned forward and spoke softly into his ear. "My name is Officer Meyers and you're under arrest."

Despite his other cheek grinding into the cement, he laughed—not with amusement, but shock. "You have to be kidding me."

"No joke," was her no-nonsense reply as she patted down his sides and ran her hands along the length of his legs, even checking around his ankles.

Tensing from her invasive search, he asked sharply, "What did I do?"

NOTHING. ROBBIE HAD a sinking feeling as she slid her hands into the back pockets of his faded jeans. He carried no weapon, no drugs or related paraphernalia. Only a worn leather wallet, and when she reached into the front pockets, all she pulled out was a ring of keys. Her palms damp with nerves, she flipped open the wallet to read his ID. Holden Thomas.

"Are you Reverend Thomas?" she asked.

His wasn't the male voice that responded, though. The vice sergeant, undercover in ratty jeans and a flannel shirt, rushed up and asked, "God, Robbie, why'd you hook up the reverend?"

"I—I didn't know…" The bust had gone down so fast and shots had been fired. When he'd reached for her she'd dropped him—to protect herself and to keep him out of the line of fire until a Special Response Team officer subdued the shooter.

Sergeant Bartholomew "Billy" Halliday, her superior officer, grabbed the youth minister's arm and helped him to his feet. "Uncuff the reverend," he ordered.

Robbie's trembling fingers fumbled the key into the lock. As she released the cuffs her fingertips brushed Thomas's wrists, and heat streaked through her, despite the brisk wind blowing in from outside. "I'm sorry," she murmured. "I thought you were a…"

"What?" he asked, turning toward her—his eyes, a startling greenish blue, narrowed in anger. "What did you think I was?"

"A dealer," she admitted.

"You thought the reverend was the guy?" Halliday asked with a gruff laugh.

"He matched the description." Robbie defended her mistake, but heat still rushed to her face.

"I'm not the guy," Holden Thomas said. A muscle twitched in his scraped cheek as he clenched his jaw.

"I know that now. I'm sorry," she said again, even as her contriteness faded to irritation. "But what are you doing here?"

Before the man could answer, Billy interrupted with

a declaration, "I got the dealer." A cocky grin creased his bearded face. He was good. That was why Halliday, who was only a year or two older than Robbie's twenty-five, had already earned the promotion to sergeant. "He's on his way to booking."

"What about the kids?" Thomas asked, his attention on the teenagers that Special Response Team members were leading off in cuffs. "What are you doing with them?"

"We're booking the ones in possession of drugs or alcohol," the sergeant explained.

"And the others?"

Billy shrugged. "We'll release them to their parents or guardians."

"And if they don't have either of those?"

"We'll call in social workers," the sergeant replied, distracted as some of the teens tried to wrestle free. "Hey, you're both good now, right? I gotta oversee the loading." With a nod at Thomas, Billy hurried back to the action.

Robbie resisted the urge to call the sergeant back. She and the youth minister were *not* good. Noting the blood smeared across his scraped cheek, she winced, and just barely refrained from offering another apology. Since he hadn't acknowledged the first two, there was no point in offering a third.

"Loading?" Thomas asked, his brow furrowed in confusion.

"Putting them in the paddy wag—in the van. This was a raid," she explained. "We bust everyone in the place on suspicion of possessing narcotics. Which brings me back to the question you didn't answer— what are you doing here?"

He gestured toward the kids in cuffs. "Looking for one of them."

"I've heard about your shelter," she said, and she'd been impressed and pleased that he had founded such a useful facility. "But I thought they came to you. I didn't know you recruited."

"Recruited?" He lowered his chin, so that their gazes met. "You think I'm encouraging kids to run away?"

She shook her head. "No, of course not. I just can't figure out why you'd come down here. Nothing good happens in this area of town." Criminals had turned the abandoned warehouses and factories in this part of Lakewood into meth labs and crack houses. "It's too dangerous."

"Too dangerous for kids," he agreed. "That's why I had to come down here. I'd heard that one of the kids from the shelter—a young girl—was coming to this party. But no one's seen her."

"It's too dangerous for anyone."

He touched a knuckle to his scraped cheek and grimaced. "I can't argue that." Then he glanced at the watch on his wrist and cursed. "I'm late. I have to go."

Disappointment tugged at Robbie, but she shrugged it off. She wasn't disappointed he was going. She was disappointed only because she couldn't leave, too. She had already wasted enough time with the youth minister; she had to help the sergeant now.

"Am I free to go?" he asked, lifting a brow above one of those greenish-blue eyes.

Heat streaked through her again, but this time it had nothing to do with embarrassment and everything to do with attraction. Maybe her best friend was right; maybe she didn't date enough. But she had someone in her life more important than a man, someone who deserved all her spare time. If only she had more...

"You're free to go," she said. But when he turned to leave, she added, "For now."

He whirled back, obviously perplexed. "For now?"

"You need to come down to the station and give your statement," she explained.

"Statement? About what?" he asked. "I already told you why I was here."

"I know, but you're a witness. We need your statement about what you saw go down tonight." She really shouldn't let him leave until he gave it, but she would rather not be the one to take it. "You can come by the station tomorrow and talk to Sergeant Halliday or the watch commander, Lieutenant O'Donnell."

"Sure, I'll do that." He touched his fingers to his cheek. "But I didn't see a whole lot...from the ground."

She couldn't help herself from saying it again. "I am sorry for—"

"Mistaking me for a drug dealer," he finished for her, his voice gruff with disgust. She had offended him even more than she suspected. No wonder he hadn't acknowledged her apologies.

She nodded. "Yeah, for that."

He glanced at his watch once more, then started walking toward the open garage door. Before jumping down from the loading dock, he turned back and admitted, "I made a mistake, too. I mistook you for a runaway."

He hadn't been mistaken, actually, but Robbie didn't enlighten him. Instead, she turned away and pushed him from her mind as she joined her fellow officers. She couldn't afford to be distracted, not in her line of work. And the only way to keep Holden Thomas from distracting her was to completely forget about him.

BECAUSE HE ARRIVED late, Holden had to stand in the back of the small auditorium and peer over the heads of the other parents to see his niece onstage as she belted out a song with the rest of her fourth-grade class. Warmth spread through his chest, tempering his earlier frustration and disappointment.

He'd been more worried about *her* disappointment than his, though. He couldn't fail her like he'd failed her mother. He closed his eyes as guilt and sorrow rushed over him, but then he forced the feelings back to focus on Lorielle's daughter.

The class sang disjointedly, their youthful voices out of sync. After only a week of school, the music teacher couldn't have expected much. But the song was only one part of the back-to-school open house. Thanks to the raid, he'd missed the beginning. As he thought of the beautiful vice officer, tension knotted his shoulders.

The woman had no idea the nerve she'd touched when she'd mistaken him for what he abhorred most. Yet she had an excuse. Only drug dealers and their customers hung out in that part of the city. He had no excuse, mistaking her for a runaway. Her undercover disguise, even if it was the current teen uniform, hadn't clothed a teenage body. Her unzipped hoodie had revealed a lacy camisole and full breasts—before those breasts had been pressed against his back when she'd leaned forward after cuffing him and identifying herself, her breath warm in his ear.

Heat flashed through him, but he blamed it on the closeness of the crowd and on his embarrassment that she'd gotten the jump on him. Despite her petite stature, the woman was strong. And she *was* a woman, more because of the look in her eyes than the curves of her body. That look hadn't reflected the suspicion of a teenager so much as the cynicism of an adult, of a *cop*.

Applause rang out around Holden, the loud sudden noise making him flinch. He shook off the flash of anxiety and clapped, too. Then, lifting his fingers to his lips, he produced a shrill whistle.

Moments later a little blond girl burst through the throng. "Uncle Holden! I heard you whistling! You made it!"

"Of course I made it," he said. He could have blamed Officer Meyers for making him late. Even now he could feel her hands patting down his body and searching his pockets. But it was his own fault. Again. "I wouldn't have missed your open house for anything."

He lifted Holly in his arms. She was small for nine, with a delicate build—like her mother had had. She looked so much like Lorielle, in fact, that he felt a twinge of pain in his chest.

The twinge moved to his cheek as Holly pressed her fingertips to it and gasped. "Uncle Holden! You're hurt."

"I'm fine," he assured her.

Her eyes widened with fear. "What happened?"

The child had spent too much of her young life worrying about the only parent she'd known—and for good reason. Since he'd become her guardian, Holden had wanted to offer her nothing but security and stability.

"You know how clumsy I am." He laughed. "I just tripped and fell, honey. That's all that happened."

"You're really okay?" she asked, a catch in her voice.

"Really," he vowed, gently tweaking her nose. "And you were fantastic. You sounded wonderful up there."

"Did you hear me?" she asked hopefully. "Really?"

He nodded. "Loud and clear." For a small girl, she had a surprisingly big voice and an even bigger presence. "Now show me around your new school."

She wriggled down from his arms, clasping his hand and tugging him through the crowd. "You have to meet my new best friend."

He smiled, silently dismissing the fears and doubts he'd had about Holly's switching schools when they'd moved into the house he'd inherited from his grandfather. He'd worried that she would have trouble making new friends, but he should have known better; should have known Holly better.

He had promised himself he wouldn't make the same mistakes with her that he had with Lorielle. Once their dad had divorced her mother, Holden hadn't had enough contact with his younger half sister. He hadn't really known her at all.

Holly stopped moving abruptly. "I found him," she said to a child as petite as she was. "This is my uncle Holden. Uncle Holden, this is my best friend, Kayla."

He leaned down to meet the dark-haired child's gaze. "I've heard so much about you, Kayla. Holly talks about you all the time."

The little girl nodded. "She's my best friend. We're going to be like my mom and Aunt JoJo. We'll be friends even when we're old, too."

He glanced up, looking for the woman whose daughter had just called her old. The auditorium was still crowded, but no one stood near them. "I'd love to meet your parents, Kayla."

"I don't have a dad," she said matter-of-factly. "It's always been just me and my mom."

He wondered if Kayla had lost a parent like Holly had, to death, or to divorce when she'd been too young to remember her father. But he wouldn't ask such personal questions of a child.

"Well, I'd love to meet your mom." He had a lot of respect for anyone who could raise a child alone. He still struggled with his own doubts and inadequacies in the parenting department, even though Holly had been living with him on and off since she was a baby, and for the past few years permanently.

"Aunt JoJo brought me, but she stepped outside to take a call on her cell. My mom's not here. She had to work." Kayla's lips formed a slight pout.

"That's too bad she didn't get off work for the open house," he said, "but I'm sure she tried."

Kayla shrugged thin shoulders. "I dunno. But it's okay. My mom's job is real important."

"What does she do?" he found himself asking, despite his reluctance to pry.

"She's a cop."

He studied the child more closely. She had long, black curls. But Officer Meyers's hair had probably been a wig, part of her disguise. Were Kayla's eyes the same shade of pale blue? Could she be...?

He shook his head in an effort to banish the image of the sexy vice cop. She was older than the teenager she had tried to pass for, but not by much. Not old enough to have a nine-year-old daughter, he would bet. And really, he should take that bet, because what were the odds of his niece's new best friend being *her* daughter?

Not great. About as great as him ever seeing Officer Meyers again. She hadn't offered to take his statement; instead, she'd told him to give it to the sergeant or watch commander. So he doubted he'd see her when he dropped by the station.

It wasn't likely she'd stop by the shelter, either. The only representatives of the Lakewood Police Department to ever stop by the shelter had been the chief, at the opening, and the public-information officer, who'd been there a few times over the past six months. Holden would have liked them to be more involved, but after tonight and the raid, he wasn't certain if their presence at the shelter would help or hurt his ability to reach skittish runaways.

He had a feeling any further contact with Officer Meyers would hurt him more than a scraped cheek and bruised shins. She'd be a distraction from what was most important to him. His niece. And the shelter.

No. What was he thinking? He wasn't attracted to Officer Meyers. She was not his type at all. He was already dating someone who was his type—exactly his type. Someone as busy as he was, with little time to devote to a relationship.

He sucked in a breath; maybe he needed to *make* time. Maybe he needed to give Holly the family he had promised his sister he would provide for her daughter.

Chapter Two

Robbie flipped a pancake onto a plate, taking care not to fold the ears. "And voilà—a breakfast fit for my singing diva!" she exclaimed as she placed the plate on the small bistro table, which was all that would fit in the tiny kitchen of their apartment.

"Mouse cakes!" Kayla exclaimed as she squirted syrup over the chocolate-chip pancake. "Thanks, Mom."

Regret tugged at the smile Robbie forced. "Aunt JoJo sent me the video she took with her phone last night. I couldn't wait to watch it." While they'd been writing up the reports for the raid, she'd slipped away to the women's room to view the footage of the performance. She'd been razzed enough over almost arresting Holden Thomas; she hadn't wanted to give them another reason to tease her by tearing up because she'd missed hearing her baby sing.

Kayla glanced up from her plate. "You saw it? What did you think?"

"You were fabulous," Robbie praised her daughter as she settled into her chair, grasping the handle of her coffee mug. She'd nearly drained the pot trying to wake up—it had been a long night. "I would've been there if I could." She already felt guilty about not working the extra shifts everyone else at Lakewood PD worked. To beg off her regular shift would have been not just irresponsible but dangerous to her fellow officers.

"I know, Mom. It's okay," Kayla assured her. "Holly's uncle was there."

Guilt caused Robbie's stomach to churn. Holly's uncle had made it and Kayla's mother, her only parent, hadn't. "That's great," she murmured through clenched teeth.

"He's really nice," her daughter said, her blue eyes bright with awe.

Maybe lack of sleep had Robbie jumping to conclusions, but she detected something more than awe, as well. Wistfulness, as if her daughter wished she had an uncle. Or a father?

"That's great…" Kayla had never seemed to mind that it was just the two of them. Had she actually been longing for more? A dad?

Kayla gave an eager nod, tousling her unruly curls even more. "He said that I can come over to their house sometime."

"He did?" From her years on the street, as a runaway and a cop, Robbie had learned to suspect everyone's motives. "Does Holly live with him?"

Her mouth full of pancake, Kayla nodded.

"What about her parents?"

The little girl swallowed hard. "She's like me and doesn't have a dad." Robbie was filled with regret, thinking that Kayla had to live with the consequences of her mother's mistakes.

"And her mom is dead," Kayla continued.

"Oh, that's terrible," Robbie said with a flash of sympathy. "I'm so sorry to hear that."

"It happened a long time ago," Kayla said with a slight shrug. "She's been living with her uncle for a while. So can I go over to their house sometime?"

"Well, how about we have Holly here first?" Robbie asked. Then she would have a chance to meet the uncle when he dropped off his niece. She'd probably even run a background check on the guy before she let her daughter spend any time at his house.

She had seen too many things, before and since she'd become a cop, to risk her daughter's safety. She told herself—and her friend Joelly, when she bugged Robbie to get out more—that Kayla's safety was also why she didn't date much. Or at all, lately.

But was she really not dating in order to protect her daughter…or herself?

HOLDEN STEPPED into the glass vestibule and pressed the intercom next to the interior doors.

"Your business?" a disembodied voice asked.

"I'm Holden Thomas," he replied, "and I'm coming in to give my statement about the—"

The intercom buzzed as the locks clicked. He opened the door and stepped into the station of the Lakewood Police Department. Sunlight poured through transom windows, sparkling off the polished terrazzo flooring and tiled walls. A bronze bust of an officer's capped head and shoulders in the middle of the lobby drew his attention to the marble wall behind the bust. Pictures of officers in uniforms from different eras had been lined up at eye level. Plaques beneath the pictures identified the men and one woman who had fallen in the line of duty.

"Reverend Thomas," a man greeted him, drawing his attention away from the memorial. "I'm Lieutenant Patrick O'Donnell." The officer, clad in the department's black uniform, held out his hand.

Holden shook it. "Pleased to meet you."

"It's great to meet you," the lieutenant said. His eyes, nearly the same reddish brown as his hair, warmed with sincerity. "I've heard wonderful things about the shelter you started."

"You should come by and check it out," Holden urged. "It'd be great to have officers stop in on a regular basis." For him. He wasn't as certain the kids would agree.

"None of Lakewood's finest have stopped by?" the lieutenant asked as he gestured for Holden to follow him behind the memorial.

"The chief came to the opening," Holden admitted, "and Sergeant Terlecki has stopped in a few times." But the kids still referred to the department's public-information officer as "the TV cop."

O'Donnell sighed and pushed a hand through his short hair. "Sorry about that. We've been pretty under-staffed lately, everyone having to pull extra shifts." He pointed to the pictures that lined the walls leading back to the reception desk. These officers wore military uniforms. "A lot of our officers have been called back to active duty."

One of the photos caught Holden's attention. "Sean O'Donnell? Is he a relative?"

"My younger brother," the lieutenant replied with pride. "He's been back a few years, but he did a couple tours. Special Ops. Now he's a member of the Special Response Team. He was at the raid last night."

Holden studied the picture of the red-haired soldier but didn't recognize him. The only one he remembered was Officer Meyers. Unfortunately he remembered her too well.

"Thanks for coming down to give your statement," O'Donnell said, "since Officer Meyers didn't take it at the scene."

"That's my fault." Holden defended her although he doubted she needed anyone protecting her, given the ease with which she'd taken him down. "I was late for something important."

"You're lucky you made it at all," O'Donnell remarked as he led the way around the reception desk to a glass-walled office behind it.

Holden followed him and settled into the chair O'Donnell indicated. "What do you mean? Are you talking about Officer Meyers nearly arresting me?"

O'Donnell chuckled. "I'm talking about her saving your life."

"Saving my life?"

"You heard the shots, right?"

Holden nodded as he remembered the explosion of noise. "Yeah, it all happened so quickly."

"The Special Response Team sergeant said that if Roberta hadn't knocked you down, you'd probably have worse than a few scrapes and bruises."

Holden sucked in a breath of surprise. "Really?"

"The SRT sergeant wrestled the gun from the kid

who pulled it, but not before the kid got off some wild shots."

The shelter wasn't far from the warehouse; Holden had founded it in the neighborhood that needed it most. So he was used to hearing gunfire. "I hadn't realized how close it was."

"It's a dangerous area, Reverend."

"That's what Officer Meyers said."

"She'd know." Something about the lieutenant's tone suggested that he was referring to more than her knowledge as a police officer. "So what is your recollection of last night?"

"It's very limited," he admitted. "I came to the warehouse to stop a girl from getting into trouble. But I couldn't find her." He'd found Officer Meyers, instead.

"She wasn't there?" O'Donnell asked, his fingers on the keyboard of the laptop open on his desk. "Did you recognize anyone else?"

Holden shrugged, not wanting to get anyone in trouble. The kids trusted him. And thankfully the ones he'd recognized had left right before the raid. "I'm not sure. Some faces looked familiar, but I don't know any of their names."

"Did you think you recognized Officer Meyers?" O'Donnell prodded. "Is that why you approached her?"

"I thought she was a kid," Holden admitted. "I thought she needed help." Instead, she'd been the one to help him, and he hadn't even realized it.

"She did. We are short-staffed," O'Donnell reminded him with a quick grin. "Do you remember what happened after that?"

"The SWAT team rushed in—"

"SRT," O'Donnell corrected him.

"The music was cut off. Men were shouting. Then the shots were fired," he said. "I didn't really see anything. Will I need to testify?"

"That would be up to the assistant district attorney," O'Donnell said. "But I doubt it."

Holden sighed. "I guess I wouldn't be much help. I didn't even realize what was going on."

"It would help *you,* at the shelter, if you understood more about police procedure," O'Donnell suggested. "You'd be able to explain exactly what's going to happen to those kids if they get into trouble."

"Yeah," Holden agreed. "That's why it would be great to have more officers stop by."

"I'd like to promise you some Lakewood PD volunteers," O'Donnell said, "but we have to worry about covering shifts and still having enough time for sleep and to check in with our families."

"Now *that* I do understand." Time management was something Holden had yet to master himself.

"Yeah, you're busy." O'Donnell shook his head and chuckled. "It was a crazy idea."

"What was a crazy idea?"

"The CPA—Citizens' Police Academy," the lieutenant replied. "Well, *that's* not the crazy idea. It's a great program that gives citizens an inside look at the police department. It's been great for promoting community involvement. Your joining it was the crazy idea."

"Why?" The idea actually intrigued Holden.

"You have no time."

He expelled a ragged sigh. "You're right. I don't have the time."

"But, you know, it only meets one night a week," O'Donnell said. "Wednesday nights from six-thirty to ten."

"For how many weeks?"

"Fifteen."

Fifteen weeks. Holly had grown used to the crazy hours he kept, leaving at all hours of the night to drop in at the shelter. The nanny, Mrs. Crayden, was always there for her, so his niece was never alone or neglected. Still, Holden felt as if he was letting her down, as if he was never there for her—as he hadn't been there for her mother when *she* had needed him.

"That many weeks?" He shook his head. "I don't think I can make that kind of commitment." No matter how much he wanted to.

"You understand commitment," the lieutenant said. "You left St. Mike's Youth Center and opened up the shelter on your own. That was quite a commitment."

Holden nodded, his temples throbbing with his old worry that he'd taken on too much. Not financially; he had barely touched the inheritance from his grandfather that he'd used to found and run the shelter. It was time he was lacking.

"If you can't complete the course, that's fine," O'Donnell assured him. "You can drop out. Some people have had to drop out of every session. Life sometimes gets in the way."

Life and death. He'd had to drop out of the seminary, in order to take care of Holly. But because he'd completed his masters in psychology and theology, St. Michael's had hired him as a youth minister. He wasn't really the reverend that everyone called him, though.

"So when does the academy start?" he asked.

"Wednesday," O'Donnell reminded him with a laugh. "Tonight."

"WHAT ARE YOU doing here?" Billy Halliday asked as Robbie slid into the seat next to him at the table at the front of the third-floor conference room. "It's your day off."

"He's no saint," Robbie whispered.

"Who? Paddy's never claimed sainthood."

Watch Commander Lieutenant Patrick "Paddy" O'Donnell had just briefed them and the several other officers gathered at that table for the first class, or intro session, of the Citizens' Police Academy.

"I wasn't talking about Paddy," she said. Then the man about whom she'd spoken walked into the room. "I was talking about the man you call the patron saint of runaways."

"Reverend Thomas," Billy said with a wave at the youth minister.

"He's not even a real reverend," she went on. "He dropped out of seminary college. All he has is a master's degree in adolescent psychology."

"You ran a background check on him?"

"Of course." She'd wanted to make sure the teenagers were safe around him. She knew from personal experience that those kids were prey for dangerous people such as drug dealers and sexual predators.

"So does he have a criminal record?" Billy asked.

"No," she admitted with a contrary flash of disappointment. She should have been happy that he might actually be that saint everyone thought him to be. Those kids could certainly use one.

"So what's your problem with him?"

"I think when he gave his statement to Paddy, he complained about me," Robbie said, nerves getting the better of her. Just nerves. She was *not* reacting to how handsome Holden Thomas looked in a black sweater and faded jeans, his hair mussed as if he'd been running his hands through it.

"Why? About what?" Billy asked, outraged on her behalf. "You saving him from getting his head blown off?"

She smiled at her superior officer's protectiveness but shook her head. "I doubt he would have gotten hit if I hadn't tripped him. *I'm* the reason he got hurt. He must have said something to Paddy and that's why I got 'recruited' to help out with the CPA." Recruited by a quick telephone summons to show up tonight for class.

"Paddy probably just wants all the help he can get," Billy said, turning his gaze to another dark-haired woman sitting at the table closest to the officers. The reporter for the Lakewood *Chronicle* had been the first to arrive, as if she'd thought she might have had to fight her way into the building.

"I can't believe Paddy let Erin Powell into the program," Robbie remarked, "with some of the stuff she's written about the department."

"Kent Terlecki okayed her joining the CPA," Billy said. "And she's been a lot harder on him than on the rest of the department in her articles." Billy shook his head, as if bewildered by his housemate's behavior—he and the public-information officer rented a house together. "Hell, I guess he thinks the CPA might change her mind."

Robbie shrugged. "It's hard to improve bad press," she said as she met Joelly Standish's gaze from across

Once a Cop

the room. The media had painted her friend as a spoiled debutante just because she was the mayor's daughter. They had no idea about the kind of selfless person she'd always been, despite her sometimes overbearing father. Of course part of that was Joelly's fault—she liked playing the bad girl for the press, knowing it annoyed her father. The mayor kind of deserved whatever embarrassment his daughter caused him—at least for the past year when he'd been going after the Lakewood PD, trying to cut their budget because of some vendetta he had against the chief. That was why Joelly had joined the CPA, so that she could use what she learned about the department to get her father to back off.

Since Joelly was fully aware that most of the residents of Lakewood regarded her as an indulged princess and knew about the animosity between the police department and her father, she had insisted that Robbie not acknowledge their friendship in case it caused problems for her. But Joelly would not be a problem. No, if anyone was going to be a problem for her, it was Holden Thomas. Robbie's gaze slid from Joelly to him.

Goose bumps lifted her skin as she realized he'd been staring at her. She hated that she found him so attractive; the last time she'd fallen in love she'd wound up living on the streets, pregnant and alone. Even though there was no risk of that happening again, now that she was older and wiser, there was also no risk of her falling in love again. Since she was older and wiser.

Holden couldn't believe he'd actually returned tonight for a meeting of the Citizens' Police Academy. What had he been thinking? He didn't have time for this. Sure, he'd like to learn more about police procedures. It would help him deal with kids at his shelter when they complained about the police hassling them.

Or did he just want to learn more about *her?*

If not for her light blue eyes and pale skin, he wouldn't have recognized Robbie. In the black Lakewood PD uniform, she looked so different from the sexily dressed woman of the night before. Even her hair had been subdued, pulled back in a thick braid that hung down her back.

She didn't speak until the lead instructor of the CPA, Lieutenant O'Donnell, introduced the officers who would teach sessions of the program. "Sergeant Bartholomew Halliday and Officer Roberta Meyers will teach the course on the vice unit."

"I don't need help learning new vices," an older man sitting next to Holden quipped. Then color rushed to his face. "Sorry, Reverend."

During the class introductions, Holden had learned the man, Donald Baker, was a neighborhood-watch captain. The class of nearly twenty included a few neighborhood-watch captains and a vast assortment of other citizens: two teachers, some college students, a reporter, an older married couple and a former gang member who'd begun his own community-outreach program, an after-school youth center for kids at risk of joining gangs. He was in great company. Holden grinned, silently assuring Baker that he'd taken no offense.

Officer Meyers stepped up to the podium. The mike screeched as she adjusted it to her height. Then she cleared her throat and said, "We look forward to sharing with you our experiences as undercover vice officers."

The memory of her, in those ripped jeans and that tight camisole, kept flitting through his mind, distracting him from the class, so that he was startled when, some time later, everyone started to file out of the meeting room.

"Glad you decided to join us," a familiar male voice welcomed him.

Holden glanced up at Sergeant Billy Halliday. Roberta Meyers stood silently at the lanky man's side. "I'm not really sure why I'm here," he said. He needed to thank her for saving him the other night; however, the words stuck in his throat.

"No burning desire to learn more about law enforcement?" she asked.

"No," Holden said and hoped like heck he spoke the truth. "No burning desire."

"Then why are you here?" she asked.

The sergeant gasped as if surprised at her bluntness, but Holden suspected she always lacked finesse. He shrugged. "I guess I'd like to learn more about what happened last night—about why. Then maybe I can explain it to my kids." He grinned. "Or convince some of Lakewood PD's finest to explain it to them."

Officer Meyers chuckled. "Doesn't matter who talks to them—good luck getting them to listen."

"I think they'd listen to a police officer." At least they would if Holden could find one who knew how to reach them.

"I work undercover a lot," Billy pointed out, rubbing his shaggy beard. "I'm going under tonight again, but I'll definitely stop by when I'm between assignments. And I'll make sure some other officers come by, as well."

"Thanks," Holden said, his own tension easing. Maybe joining the Citizens' Police Academy hadn't been a mistake, after all.

"Sure thing," Halliday said, then glanced toward the door. "Uh, my mom's waiting for me…"

Holden held in a chuckle, seeing the irritation and embarrassment on the vice cop's face. He'd also caught the man's look of surprise earlier, when his mother had walked in and explained that she'd joined the program to learn more about her son's job—since she could never get any information out of him.

Roberta Meyers stared at the retreating sergeant, then met Holden's gaze. Her pupils widened, nearly eclipsing the icy-blue irises.

"What about you, Officer?" he asked. "Will you help out at the shelter?"

She shook her head.

"Not interested in giving back to the community?"

A breath hissed out between her lips. "I give back to the community by doing my job."

"Your job is really important to you," he surmised.

"Of course."

"And mine is really important to me," he said. Although he didn't consider the shelter a job; it was so much more than that. Sometimes a vocation. Sometimes a penance. "Helping those kids really matters to me."

"I help them, too," she insisted, her tone defensive, "by getting the drug dealers and other predators off the streets."

He uttered a soft whistle in appreciation of the work she did. "I guess you're doing more than I am."

"Your shelter is vital," she assured him. "The kids need it…and you."

Again he got the impression she knew that personally, and not just because of her job. So he implored her, "Come by the shelter and talk to them."

Somehow he suspected they would connect with her a lot better than they had with the TV cop.

"You really want me to work with you?" she asked, her eyes narrowed with suspicion.

"Only for the sake of the kids," he hastened to explain. "I think you could relate to them." And he wanted to know *how* she could do that. He wanted to know entirely too much about her.

"I don't have the time."

He should have been relieved. He really shouldn't want to spend more time with the cynical cop. And even if she could relate to the kids, that didn't mean she'd be able to help them. Especially since she obviously wasn't willing to take on the task.

With a brief nod, she walked from the room—as if proving her claim that she had no time. Holden stared after her, wondering if maybe the problem wasn't the shelter. Maybe the problem was him.

Had she mistaken his request for a personal interest in her? He almost ran after her—to correct her misconception. He was already dating a woman who was perfect for him; he had no interest in Roberta Meyers.

Absolutely no interest at all.

Chapter Three

"You should stop by his shelter," Joelly said, leaning against the butcher-block kitchen counter as she sipped from her mug of coffee. "You need to check it out. I think it would be good for you." She lowered her voice to a whisper and added, "I think *he* would be good for you."

Robbie laughed at her relentless friend. "Give it up, Jo. I'm not interested."

Joelly raised her honey-blond brows. "Really? Have you seen him?"

"Seen him." She shrugged as if unimpressed, and then the devil made her add, "Felt him up, too."

Joelly sputtered, choking on her coffee. After wiping her eyes and mouth, she exclaimed, "Rob!"

Robbie laughed again. "I'm kidding. I just frisked him," although she had appreciated the curve of his tight butt when she'd slid her hands into his pockets. "During the raid—I told you about it."

"Yes, you did. And you don't usually tell me about your busts," Joelly reminded her. "You're interested in Holden Thomas."

Robbie shook her head. "No. I'm not." No matter how perfect the man seemed. She picked some used napkins off the counter, which was cluttered with ice-cream bowls and pizza plates from last night's feast, and tossed them into the trash. "I don't have the time or the energy to date."

"That's a cop-out and you know it," Joelly accused her. "You're scared because of the mistake you made a long time ago. Don't you think it's time you got back on that horse?"

Robbie glanced through the archway to the living room, where Kayla lay on her stomach in front of the television, watching cartoons. Giggles erupted from her and the little blond girl lying beside her on the hardwood floor.

"The things I've done that other people consider mistakes usually turn out to be the best things that have ever happened to me," she reminded her friend.

Joelly turned toward her goddaughter and then smiled at Robbie. "Exactly."

Robbie tossed one of the dirty napkins at Joelly's face. It struck her nose and then dropped into her mug. With a glare, Jo lifted out the dirty paper and tossed it into the trash.

More giggles erupted in the living room.

"Setting a great example," Jo accused her.

"They're laughing at the cartoons," Robbie said. The last thing she wanted was to set a bad example for her daughter. That was one reason she hadn't dated in a while; she'd never had the greatest judgment when it came to men.

As if Joelly read Robbie's mind—and maybe she had—she said, "Holden's a really great guy. He's doing so much good for the community." She glanced toward the living room, then lowered her voice and added, "For kids like we once were. I wish he'd been around back then, that his shelter for runaway teens had existed when we'd needed someplace safe to stay."

Robbie shivered as she remembered being cold and scared. And alone, until she'd met Joelly. "Yeah, the shelter's great."

"*He's* great."

Robbie shook her head. "There's something about him…" Something that unsettled her, that had her every instinct screaming to be careful. "I don't quite trust him."

"You don't trust anyone, my friend."

"I trust you." Just Joelly. Robbie had learned, the hard way, to trust no one else. Even her own parents had let her down when she'd needed them most. Not to mention the boy who'd sworn he would love her forever.

"Since you trust me, do what I tell you to do," Joelly urged, her voice and gaze stern. She put on what she called her Mean Mommy face and said, "Stop by the shelter."

"Are you sure you're not a mother?" Robbie asked. Ever since they'd first met on the streets, Joelly, despite being a year younger than Robbie, had been taking care of her.

She grinned. "I *am* a mother."

"A dog doesn't count."

"Sassy is my baby," Joelly insisted, tilting her head. "And I think she's calling me now."

Robbie listened, but couldn't hear any yelping from the Chihuahua in the next apartment. Of course the walls were thick in the old house, which had been converted into four units—Robbie and Joelly leased the downstairs ones, which were separated by the foyer. So there was no way Joelly could have heard Sassy unless she'd left her door open again. "You just don't want to help me clean up from the slumber party."

"That, too." Taking her cup with her, Joelly waggled her fingers. "Gotta go."

"We can help you with the dishes, Miss Meyers," Holly offered as she bounded into the kitchen.

Robbie envied the child's exuberance. None of them had gotten much sleep last night, but Holly hadn't needed caffeine to recover. Robbie had to pour herself another cup. "I appreciate the offer, but I'm sure your uncle will be here soon."

The other two girls who'd slept over had already been picked up. More than an hour ago.

"He probably got busy and forgot," Holly said matter-of-factly.

A pang of sympathy struck Robbie at the thought that the child considered herself so unimportant to her guardian. "I'm sure he could never forget about you." She dropped to her knees and pulled the little girl into a quick embrace. "I know I could never forget about you."

"He does," Holly said with an unconcerned shrug, "when he gets busy. That's why Mrs. Crayden lives with us."

Mrs. Crayden, the child's nanny, had dropped her off the previous evening. The older woman had been happy because, in addition to the night off, her employer had given her the rest of the weekend off. Had Holly's busy uncle figured he had a cheap replacement for the nanny in Robbie?

She wouldn't mind having the child stay—Holly

was as special as Kayla had said. Robbie had had so much fun playing games with the girls last night and this morning. Sometimes she wished Kayla wasn't an only child, but if Robbie wanted a bigger family she'd have to start dating again. And Joelly had been right about one thing—Robbie was scared to take the chance of making another mistake.

"Why don't you give me your uncle's number and I'll call and remind him?" Robbie offered.

"I don't want to bother him," Holly said. "What he does is really important, too. Like your job."

Robbie suppressed her inclination to interrogate the child. She knew little about Holly's uncle, but she would save her questions for the man himself—if he ever decided to show up.

"Holly can stay, can't she?" Kayla asked after she shut off the TV in the living room and joined them.

"Of course," Robbie assured the girls. "It's been great to finally meet your best friend." Relief eased her irritation. She was so glad that her shy daughter had met someone who'd brought her out of her shell. "Holly can stay as long as she likes."

The girls threw their arms around each other. "Yay!"

"Until her uncle comes for her," Robbie clarified, suspecting both girls would be thrilled if Holly could stay indefinitely.

"I might be here a long time," the little blonde warned her.

Robbie's annoyance with the missing uncle returned. When he finally showed up for his niece, she intended to give him a piece of her mind. As if on cue, the doorbell rang.

"That's probably Uncle Holden now," Holly said.

Holden? Realization dawned, tightening the muscles in Robbie's stomach. Holly's last name was Thomas. Holden Thomas was standing at her door?

"I'll let him in," Robbie said. "Kayla, why don't you show Holly your DVD player? Your favorite movie is probably still in it."

She waited until the girls disappeared down the short hall off the kitchen before she opened the door. Holden Thomas, hand outstretched toward the bell, drew back, his greenish-blue eyes widening with shock. In worn jeans and a jersey, he was dressed pretty much as he'd been the first time she'd seen him—when she'd slid her hands into those denim pockets and frisked him.

"I should have put it together," he murmured. "Kayla Meyers. Robbie Meyers."

"Roberta," she corrected him automatically, not wanting any familiarity between them. "I should have put it together, too."

How many different women *was* Roberta Meyers? Holden wondered. He'd met the sexy vice cop in her tight teenage outfit, then the no-nonsense police officer in her austere black uniform and tightly bound braid, and now he was meeting another version. *Mom.* She wore a baggy, black Lakewood PD sweatshirt with faded jeans. Her bare toes peeked from beneath the frayed cuffs and her thick black hair spilled out of a clip on the back of her head. She looked even younger than she had in her vice disguise.

He shook his head in stunned disbelief. "You're really old enough to have a nine-year-old?"

She nodded, but didn't share her age with him. She

couldn't have been much older when she'd had Kayla than Lorielle had been when Holly was born. Had Roberta brought her child into the world all alone, the way his sister had? Kayla had said she didn't have a dad. Had the little girl's father ever been in the picture?

Holden glanced around the small apartment, which had the same high ceilings, ornate trim and gleaming hardwood floors as the house, just a few blocks west, that he had inherited from his grandfather. Robbie's unit was small, its kitchen tucked into what had probably once been a closet. The place was only big enough for the two of them.

"I met Kayla at the back-to-school open house," he said. "She's a very sweet girl."

"Holly is, too."

Despite everything his niece had been through. Guilt weighed on him over the past and the present. "I'm sorry I'm late," he said. "Where is Holly?"

He wanted to thank Roberta for saving his neck earlier in the week, but he didn't want Holly to hear about the danger in which he'd put himself. He knew he should have thanked Roberta the other night, after the CPA class, but she'd taken him aback with her refusal to visit the shelter.

"The girls are in Kayla's room," she informed him. "I wanted to talk to you alone first."

His pulse leapt, then steadied, and he reminded himself that she didn't appear to like him much.

She gestured toward the coffeepot on the short kitchen counter. "Would you like some?" she asked.

He shook his head. "Was there a problem last night?" Holly had had nightmares, frequently, until about a year ago. Maybe sleeping in a strange place had brought all that insecurity back for her.

"No, Holly was fine. The girls had fun," she said with a smile, "and so did I." But then she added, "It was something she said this morning that concerns me. She thinks you forget about her."

He winced. "I didn't forget about her. I just got held up."

"Like you did the other night?"

Heat rushed to his face as he remembered how easily she'd caught him off guard. After all the years he'd spent dealing with surly and sometimes dangerous teenagers, he should have developed quicker reflexes. "No, I almost got arrested the other night."

"I wouldn't have booked you," she said.

He blew out an exaggerated breath of relief. "That's good."

"You had nothing in your possession that I could have used as evidence."

He assured her, "The last thing you would ever find on me is drugs."

"That's good," she said, "since you're Holly's sole guardian."

"So you know I have custody of her?" What else had his niece told her?

She nodded. "Kayla said that Holly's mother died a few years ago. She was your sister?"

Even now, nearly three years later, his heart still contracted with pain over the senseless death of his beautiful younger half sister. "Yes."

"So you're raising Holly alone?" she asked. "Your parents aren't involved? Or Holly's father?"

"You ask a lot of questions, Officer Meyers. I could

ask some of my own," he warned her, suspecting she wouldn't appreciate his prying into her life any more than he appreciated her doing the same to him. "What about Kayla's father? She says she doesn't have one. What happened to him?"

"We're not talking about Kayla," she said. "We're talking about Holly and your habit of forgetting about her. Do you have any idea how that must make her feel?"

"You've only spent a few hours, awake, with Holly. You don't know how she feels." Holden hoped he did; he hoped his niece told him the truth when she assured him that she understood about the shelter taking so much of his time. Was she old enough to understand that he was doing it for her, to honor her mother's memory?

"Do you know how she feels?" Robbie asked, as if she'd read his thoughts—and known his worry. "Young girls are sensitive. You need to be more careful with her feelings."

"And why do you think you're qualified to give me parenting advice?" he wondered aloud. "You're the one who missed your daughter's back-to-school open house."

Color rushed to her face, painting her pale skin bright pink. "I had to work."

"Since you're the one putting your job ahead of your daughter, I think you're the one who needs to be reminded of her responsibilities."

"H-how dare you," she sputtered, her eyes hard with anger.

"The same way you dare, Roberta."

"ARE THEY STILL arguing?" Kayla asked Holly, who had her ear pressed to the crack of the bedroom door. Because Kayla's room was small and filled with her canopy bed and a mirrored dresser her mother had stenciled with flowers, she stood only a few steps away from the door herself. She heard only a rumble of voices from the living room, though.

Her friend turned back and sighed. "Yes."

"Are you sure?" Kayla asked, nerves fluttering in her stomach as she thought of the *plan* she and Holly had formed last night after the other two girls had fallen asleep.

Holly's green eyes sparkled. "It's perfect."

"It *would* be perfect," Kayla cautioned, "if they go for it." If they go for each other.

"Uncle Holden is single. Well, there's this lady he sometimes goes out with, but I don't think they really *like* each other. What about your mom?"

"She doesn't ever date," Kayla admitted reluctantly. Was it her fault her mom never went out? Because if she wasn't working, she wanted to be with Kayla?

"So they're both single," Holly said as if that was all that mattered.

But Kayla was nine. And sometimes she listened to Aunt JoJo's radio show when she was supposed to be sleeping, so she knew better. She knew relationships were complicated, that it took more than two single people to make a couple. "It doesn't look—well, sound—like they like each other," she pointed out.

Holly uttered a small sigh of frustration. "But they'd be perfect for each other."

Kayla smiled. "It would be perfect for us."

Holly smiled, too. "Yeah. Mrs. Crayden's nice, but

I'd like a real mom." Her smile changed to a frown. "I barely remember mine anymore."

Kayla pulled her friend into a tight hug, her heart aching for the other girl's loss. "I'm sorry."

A small hand patted her back as if Kayla needed comforting, too. "It's okay. I have Uncle Holden. He's really more than an uncle—he's like my dad."

Kayla had to take her friend's word for it. She had never known her father. Mom had explained that he'd been too young to be a dad, but Mom must have been young, too, when she'd become a mother. "I'd like a dad," she admitted.

"And I want a mom. But more than that, I want a sister," Holly said, her arms tightening for a moment before she released Kayla. "You're going to be my sister."

"How?"

"When Uncle Holden marries your mom, he'll adopt you and she'll adopt me. And we'll become sisters."

"But how will we get them to stop fighting?" Kayla asked, lowering her voice to a whisper as she pressed her ear to the crack of the door.

No angry words drifted down the hall. In fact, she heard nothing now. Mom had to be really mad to quit talking completely. Kayla sympathized with Mr. Thomas because she hated getting the silent treatment.

"We have to make sure they spend a lot of time together," Holly said, nibbling at her lower lip as she plotted. "The more time they spend together, the more they'll see how perfect they are for each other."

Holly didn't know her mom like Kayla knew her mom. Mom always said that they didn't need a man in their lives. It was going to take a lot more than time alone to get her to change her mind.

ROBERTA COVERED her face with her hands as her shoulders shook.

"Are you crying?" Holden asked, his voice rough with unease.

She slid her palms down her face and let the laughter sputter out. "No. I'm not crying." She couldn't remember the last time she'd given in to tears.

"Why are you laughing?" he asked, almost as horrified as if she *had* been sobbing.

"Maybe lack of sleep has made me as silly as the girls," she admitted. "But do you realize how ridiculous we sound? We're fighting over who's the worse parent…"

"When we both live in glass houses," Holden said with a sigh.

"I'm sorry for lecturing you," Robbie apologized. "I had no right. It's none of my business." But even though she'd just met Holly Thomas, she'd already fallen for her, and she felt protective of the motherless child.

"I'm sorry, too," he said. "I shouldn't have said that…about you putting your job first. I was way out of line."

"You shouldn't have said that," she agreed. But then she had to know. "Is that what you think? That I put my job before my daughter?"

Holden shook his head, but before Robbie could breathe a sigh of relief, he said, "I don't know…"

"What?"

"I don't know you, Roberta." He stepped forward, standing so close that she backed against the kitchen counter. He stared into her eyes, his own eyes narrowing as he studied her. "Somehow I suspect very few people do."

She lifted her shoulders in a nonchalant shrug. "My life's an open book. I have no secrets." Joelly was the one with the secret life, not her.

He lifted a brow. "No secrets?"

She shook her head even as foreboding lifted the hair on her nape. She was going to regret that declaration, she just knew it.

"Then tell me about Kayla's father," he challenged her.

"Simple." She shrugged again. "She doesn't have one."

"The stork brought her?"

She laughed again. "If only. Then I wouldn't have had to endure twenty-three hours of labor."

He grimaced in apparent commiseration. "Twenty-three? My sister was in labor for sixteen, and I thought that was bad enough."

"You were with her?" Robbie had had no family at her side—only Joelly, who'd been as scared as she'd been.

Holden must have caught the wistfulness in her voice because now he focused on her again, his gaze intense. "You were alone?"

"I had a friend with me."

"Not your parents? But you must have been a teenager when you had Kayla."

She nodded. "Sixteen. My folks weren't too happy when I turned up pregnant." She glanced down the short hall to Kayla's closed door. "While that's no secret, this might not be the best time or place for this discussion."

"You're right," he agreed readily, as if he hadn't really been interested, after all. "I should get Holly and go. You must be exhausted from the slumber party."

"Thanks," she said.

"For what?"

"For letting me know I look like hell." She no doubt had dark circles beneath her eyes. Self-consciously she touched the clip, from which most her hair had fallen.

"You don't," he said. His deep voice dropped to a whisper as he added, "I don't think you could."

Robbie nearly choked on the breath that backed up in her lungs and throat. Her pulse quickened, and her heart raced. It had to be from all the caffeine she'd chugged that morning, not from the appreciative gleam in his eyes. She licked her lips and managed to reply, "Thank you."

"I'm the one who should be thanking you," he said.

A giggle slipped out. And she never giggled. "For what? The lecture I gave you?"

"For saving my life the other night."

She laughed again. "You'd probably have gotten hurt less if you'd taken your chances with the bullets."

She lifted her fingertips to his cheek. The scrape had scabbed over and the flesh beneath it was bruised, but the injury took nothing away from his devastating good looks. Her fingertips tingled from the contact with his skin. "I'm sorry you got hurt."

"You were right. I had no business being there." He leaned closer. "And I have no business doing this."

His lips touched hers, as tentatively and gently as she'd touched his cheek.

"DON'T YOU THINK Miss Meyers is pretty?" Holly asked, kneeling on a stool pulled up to the kitchen counter. She'd propped her elbows on the dark granite surface and held her chin in her hands, staring up at him. Her interest in his response was far too intense for a casual question.

"I hadn't noticed," Holden lied blatantly, even though he could still taste Roberta on his lips. What the heck had he been thinking, kissing her with the kids just a closed door away? Thank God they hadn't walked out and caught them. How would he have been able to explain what he didn't understand himself?

How could he be attracted to Roberta Meyers? Sure, she was beautiful, but she also had a job that put her life in danger. She'd actually laughed about getting shot at…

"She's really more than pretty," Holly persisted. "More like beautiful. I wish I had black hair and blue eyes like she and Kayla have."

"You're beautiful just the way you are," he assured his niece, surprised that she'd already started worrying about her appearance. But then, she'd be a teenager before he knew it. Because he dealt with teens every day, he knew that Holly would need an adult female in her life in whom she felt close enough to confide. She needed a mom.

"I asked you a question," his niece persisted. "Do you think Miss Meyers is pretty?"

A grin tugged at his lips. "I answered you." Obviously he hadn't given her the answer she'd wanted.

"How could you *not* notice what she looks like?" Holly asked, her green eyes narrowed in suspicion; it reminded him of how Roberta Meyers looked at him. "You two talked for a long time."

But he hadn't really found out anything about her

except how sweet she tasted. He didn't know why she, a single mother, would choose a career as risky as law enforcement. As he recalled the memorial wall in the lobby of the police department, he sliced through the bread on which he'd been attempting to spread peanut butter.

"Here, let me do it," Holly said, grabbing the knife from his hand. She was already so independent. But she needed people in her life on whom she could rely. Guilt gripped him. People who didn't forget about her, not that he actually had. But she deserved more. She deserved the family her mother had wanted her to have.

He had promised his sister on her deathbed that he would provide her daughter with a loving family and a stable home life—something Lorielle had always longed for. When their father had divorced her mother Holden had lost touch with his younger sibling for a long time. Eventually he had lost her completely. He had failed her.

And if he even considered finding Holly a mother who risked her life every day at work, he would fail her again. No, he shouldn't have kissed Roberta Meyers. For so many reasons…

Chapter Four

I do not put my job before my daughter. Even though he'd apologized for saying so, Robbie still reeled from Holden's accusation. And from his kiss.

He'd apologized for that, too, pulling away before she could reach for him. Not that she *would* have reached for him. She had *not* wanted that kiss.

And she did not want to be here, where she would undoubtedly see him again—at the second session for the Citizens' Police Academy. She wanted to be home, instead, with Kayla.

Of course her daughter and probably the college student who babysat her would both be asleep by now. But sometimes Robbie just stood in the doorway to Kayla's room and watched her sleep, wishing she could see the dreams passing through her daughter's head and make them all come true.

She glanced around the third-floor conference room where the class and the officer guides had just returned from a tour of the department. Fortunately she'd been late and so hadn't had to play tour guide. She spotted Holden standing next to the man who ran an after-school community center for at-risk kids. As if he'd felt her watching him, he turned and met her gaze. But then he quickly looked away again, returning his attention to Rafe Sanchez.

Did he regret that brief kiss as much as she did? Had it kept him awake the past few nights, too? She'd missed so much sleep that when they dimmed the lights to show traffic-stop videos, she nearly nodded off.

Lieutenant Chad Michalski, the department's emergency-vehicle-operation expert, introduced the traffic footage. He even showed a video of himself pulling over a student in the class. The blond saleswoman smiled as the other students and a couple of the officers teased her about trying to flirt her way out of the ticket the lieutenant had given her. Then he showed some more serious footage, of officers injured in the line of duty. Despite the dim light, Robbie could see that Holden was staring at her, instead of the projection screen. And she wondered about the look on his handsome face. Horror? Regret?

When Lieutenant Michalski finished answering questions about the traffic videos, he called a break. Robbie needed some caffeine, but Holden was standing at the back of the conference room, near the coffee carafes. So she stayed where she was.

"You going to take this?" Billy asked, drumming his fingers on the officers' table to catch her attention.

Startled, she glanced up at the sergeant. "What?"

"Do you want to introduce the vice videos and then answer any questions about them?" Billy asked. "They're coming up after the break."

"Uh," she stammered, "I—I don't know which videos you picked, so I don't think I could."

Billy lifted his wrist and glanced at his watch. "I really gotta get back to work. I'm sure you can handle this, Rob. Just wing it."

"Everybody, take your seats," Lieutenant Patrick O'Donnell commanded. "Now we're going to check out some footage of vice arrests. Officer Roberta Meyers will answer any questions you may have about what you see."

So Billy had already cleared it with Paddy, never mind that he hadn't asked her first. She turned from the watch commander back to Billy, but he'd already headed for the door and snapped off the lights on his way out. Her instincts warned her that she wasn't going to like what was about to be shown on the screen at the front of the room.

This is not going to go well...

Holden studied Roberta's face as she turned toward the screen. She looked even paler in the faint light, her jaw tight with tension.

"You're under arrest," Robbie said.

He tensed in reaction, wondering for a moment what he'd done this time. Then he realized her voice had come from the speakers of the computer projecting her image onto the screen. The person she was attempting to arrest in the video wasn't as compliant as he'd been. The gangly youth whirled away from the vehicle against which he'd been leaning and advanced on Robbie, fists raised. His knuckles struck her face, and blood, thick and red, spurted from her nose and mouth.

Holden gasped in shock. Similar reactions arose from the other people in the room, and some looked away in horror. But Holden could not look away. He stared at the screen and watched as Roberta, despite her injury, managed, with the help of another officer, to subdue the violent suspect. The computer clicked, launching into another video segment, this one of Robbie frisking a suspect. Suddenly she jerked her hand from a hoodie pocket and cursed.

"Needle, Rob?" another officer asked.

She nodded, her lower lip drawn between her teeth— not in pain but fear, more fear than she'd shown when she'd been hit in the face.

Holden's guts tightened with concern, which only increased as the next video ran, showing footage of a suspect flipping out in a fast-food restaurant. When a stun gun failed to subdue him, several officers had to take the guy down. Roberta was one of them, and she didn't hesitate before piling on top of the flailing man. His fists and feet connected, but still she didn't back down.

Holden's was the first hand to go up when the lights went on. Robbie ignored him and called on Bernie Gillespie, the wife of the older couple who'd admitted to joining the program for thrills. Was that why Roberta had decided to become a police officer? Holden wondered. Was she a thrill seeker?

"Do people often underestimate you because of your size?" Bernie asked. Although short, the woman wasn't exactly petite.

Instead of meeting the woman's gaze, Roberta met Holden's and answered succinctly, "Yes."

She continued to ignore Holden's raised hand and called on Leonard Romanski, the twenty-something kid who'd told them he wanted to be a police officer. "So is vice the most dangerous unit?" he asked.

Her lips curved into a slight smile. "The answer to that question probably depends on the officer you ask. Vice is rough, there's no doubt. We deal with desperate people who are sometimes out of their minds on drugs. They have no control over their actions or themselves, so it makes it hard for us to control them—as you saw on the videos."

Knowing she was ignoring him, Holden just called out his question. "So why would someone raising a small child alone choose such an assignment?"

Color flooded Roberta's face, turning her pale skin bright pink. Obviously she wasn't thrilled that he'd shared her personal situation with the rest of the class. But she lifted her chin with pride. "We don't necessarily choose our assignments. Some officers have unique skills that make them more suitable for a certain department or field."

The watch commander, who had explained at the first class that he was responsible for handing out assignments to the officers, spoke up. "And Officer Meyers's small stature and youthful appearance makes her an effective vice decoy."

"There's no arguing that," Holden agreed ruefully.

"Officers have families," Lieutenant O'Donnell continued, "and so do the citizens we're trying to protect. Heck, so do most of the criminals we're trying to get off the streets. It's just a fact of life."

"Having a family does affect how we do our jobs," Roberta added with a pointed glance at Holden. "It makes us more determined to do our jobs well and to keep Lakewood safe for our kids. Because our families come first."

The other officers and some of the citizens applauded her response. Holden only managed a smile and a nod in acknowledgment. Robbie believed what she said, but now that Holden had seen the videos showing exactly what an officer's job was like, he knew he was right. Even though he *was* attracted to Roberta Meyers, nothing could come of that attraction. She was not the woman for him.

Less than an hour later, he reminded himself of that as he stood over Holly's bed. She'd kicked off the covers and lay on her back, sprawled across the entire double bed. Her mouth hung open, soft snores escaping from her throat.

A smile curved his lips as he watched her sleep, so peacefully now…

But he could remember those nightmares when she'd first come to live with him. The way she'd awakened, screaming in fear. For herself or her mother?

Lorielle had often been battered and bruised. Like Roberta, she'd put herself in danger. Sure, Roberta had an admirable reason; she was doing her job, trying to make the streets safe. He respected her for that, but respect was all he could ever feel for her.

He couldn't put Holly or himself through the pain and uncertainty of caring for someone who willingly risked her safety and her life. He stepped out into the hall, drawing the door partly closed behind him. Then he pulled out his cell and dialed a familiar number.

After scarcely a full ring, a woman's voice answered, "Hello."

"Meredith, I hope it's not too late to call," he began as the grandfather clock on the landing chimed midnight.

She chuckled. "Of course not. You know me, I never sleep."

His tension eased as he acknowledged exactly how well he knew Meredith Wallingford. They'd grown up together, their parents close friends who'd often joked that they would arrange a marriage between their two children. But Holden had gone off to the seminary and Merry had married someone else. They'd remained friends, though, and when she divorced they began to date. Casually. Infrequently. Neither of them having the time for anything more.

It was time to *make* time. His attraction to Roberta Meyers was just superficial. His long friendship with Meredith was much deeper, a much stronger foundation on which to build a lasting relationship. He didn't have to make the mistakes his father had to realize that.

"Holden?" she said, her voice soft with concern. "Are you all right?"

"Yes," he assured her, "I'm much better now." He'd regained his focus, his objectivity. "It's been too long since I've talked to you."

She chuckled again and reminded him, "We just talked a couple of days ago."

"About one of the kids," he said. Merry was a social worker for the city of Lakewood. "Not about us."

"Us?" she queried, her tone guarded. "Is there an us?"

"I think maybe there should be," he said.

Her response was a silence that lasted so long he wondered if he'd lost the connection.

"Merry?"

"Are you sure about this?" she asked. "We've known each other a long time."

"That's why I'm sure," he said. "We know each other. We know how busy we are."

"Too busy for anything more than an occasional dinner," she reminded him.

"How about we try lunch?" he suggested.

Her tone still guarded, she asked, "When?"

"Tomorrow." The sooner he saw her, the sooner he would forget all about Roberta Meyers and how sweet her lips had tasted. "Can you come by the shelter?"

"Sure…" But she didn't sound convinced—or particularly enthusiastic—as she said goodbye and hung up.

Of course it was late. And she was tired. Tomorrow would be better. But first he had to get through tonight. Moments later he flopped onto his back in bed and closed his eyes.

And he saw her face. Roberta's…

SOMETHING SOFT and wet brushed Robbie's cheek. "Holden," she murmured as she surfaced from a deep sleep. She shifted against the mattress. How had he gotten in?

Not that she cared. She only wanted him to kiss her— *really* kiss her this time. But instead, she got the wet tongue again across the bridge of her nose. She blinked open her eyes and stared up into a furry face. "Sassy!"

The long-haired Chihuahua swiped her tongue across Robbie's mouth. Robbie sputtered, disgusted with the slimy doggie saliva, and caught the dog.

"That's probably the most action you've gotten in a while," Joelly teased from the bedroom doorway. "Or is it? I heard you say his name."

Heat rushed to Robbie's face. "Whose name?"

Joelly mocked a throaty murmur, "Holden."

"I said hold on," Robbie lied. "I knew it was Sassy wanting to go out." The little dog wriggled free of her hands and jumped off the bed to race around Joelly's bare legs.

"I already took her out."

"How long have you been here?" Robbie asked, hoping to change the subject.

"Long enough," Joelly said, "to make coffee." She crossed the short distance to the bed and pressed a mug into Robbie's hands. "Drink up. It'll be time to wake Kayla for school pretty soon."

Sunshine filtered through the thin shades, illuminating the room and the dust particles dancing in the air. Robbie really needed to clean. But who had time? She'd rather play cards or a board game with her daughter than dust any day.

As Joelly had ordered, Robbie took a deep gulp of the coffee. The rich brew flowed down her throat, hot but not scalding. It warmed her insides, just as the sunshine warmed her outside. "Mmm, thanks," she mumbled. "I owe you."

"I'm going to collect on that," Joelly warned her as she dropped onto the bed.

Awake now, thanks to Sassy's kisses and the coffee, Robbie focused on her friend, who wore the same short skirt and tight shirt she'd worn to the CPA class. "Were you out all night?"

Jo smothered a yawn behind the back of her hand. "Not like you think."

"You're not trying to live down to your bad press

again?" Robbie asked. Jo had a habit of doing crazy things to get her dad's attention.

She shook her head. "Of course that's not what my father thinks."

"You've seen your dad?" Usually Joelly didn't visit the mayor unless she had Robbie at her side for moral support.

"I got dropped off there after work last night."

And that was Robbie's fault for borrowing her car. Her clunker was in the shop again, which was the reason she'd been late for last night's CPA class. "Are you all right?"

She waved off Robbie's concern. "It was fine, even though I woke him up. Anyhow, he reminded me about his ball. He ordered me to be there."

Robbie winced. Nothing good ever came of Joel Standish ordering around his headstrong daughter. You'd think, after twenty-four years, the guy would have figured out how to deal with his namesake. "So you're not going, of course."

"No, I'm going," Joelly matter-of-factly corrected her, "and you're going to be my date."

The coffee from which Robbie had just taken a sip burned as it traveled up the back of her nose. She coughed and sputtered, and Jo thumped her back. Through watery eyes, she glared at her friend's laughing face.

"Payback."

"Are you going to cause a scene and embarrass him?" Robbie wondered. It wouldn't have been the first time Joelly had done that in retaliation to her father's patronizing behavior.

She shook her head. "That's not my intention at all. That's why you have to be my date."

"How many times do I have to tell you," Robbie said, fighting the smile that twitched her lips, "I love you, but I'm not *in* love with you?"

"Smart-ass."

"Seriously, though, you're going?"

"Yes, I'm going to try to talk some sense into him about his vendetta against the chief."

"What is that about?" Robbie asked. "Chief Archer arresting us? That happened a lifetime ago. Just how long does your dad hold a grudge?"

"Longer than that," Joelly said with a heavy sigh. Sassy, responding to the tone, jumped onto her lap. Standing on her hind legs, she lifted her front paws as far up her mistress's chest as she could reach, hugging her. Joelly stroked the dog's back as she elaborated, "My dad's ticked off about something that happened between them back in college."

"Wow, that *is* a long time. What happened?"

"My dad's girlfriend dropped him for Frank Archer. She wound up marrying him."

"So the chief's wife used to date your father?"

Joelly nodded. "She was the love of his life. They remained friends, though, until she died last year. I think my dad actually blames the chief for her getting cancer. That's why he's been on this rampage against him." She sighed again. "I have to get him to stop."

"That's why you joined the CPA."

"And that's why I have to go to this ball. And you're going, too," Joelly ordered. She failed to recognize how often she acted like her father.

Robbie smiled. She didn't have the heart to point out the similarities between dad and daughter. Joelly wouldn't appreciate the comparison.

"If you won't be my date," Joelly continued, "how about asking Reverend Thomas? At least one of us will be dating a guy my father would approve of."

"Your father would approve of Holden?" Robbie asked. Despite the animosity between the mayor and the police department, Robbie had always respected Joel Standish. She owed him so much…

Joelly nodded. "My father makes hefty donations to the shelter."

Robbie suspected that had more to do with his daughter than the youth minister.

"Maybe I should stop by the shelter," she mused aloud. It wouldn't be easy—it never was—being reminded of the life she'd led during those awful, terrifying months when she was a teenager. But she'd had to deal with the reminder more than once, since working in vice had forced her to return to the seedy district of Lakewood.

"Invite him," Joelly encouraged her.

Joelly could be bossy, but she was often right. Robbie needed to get over her fear of dating. She needed to ask Holden Thomas out.

Chapter Five

Hands clasped, heads bowed, the teenagers recited the words of Holden's favorite prayer, seeking guidance and wisdom from a higher power. Satisfaction filled him as he studied the group who'd pulled their chairs into a loose circle. These kids weren't here because their parents had forced them or bribed them, unlike most of the kids who'd been part of his youth group at St. Mike's. Contrary to Officer Meyers's remark about Holden recruiting them, these runaway teens came to the shelter of their own volition.

His satisfaction ebbed away as he acknowledged that fear and desperation were their primary motivations. But they were here—not out on the streets or in some abandoned warehouse that drug dealers had taken over. That was why he'd founded the shelter. Well, at least that was part of the reason.

Chairs creaked and rubber soles squeaked against the floor as the group dispersed. "Hey, everyone, remember to make smart choices out there," he advised as they all headed out the door, except for one girl who hung back.

"I'm sorry," she said, swinging her blond hair over her shoulder.

"About?"

"I know you went to that party last week looking for me," Skylar said, gesturing toward the scrape that had faded to a faint yellow bruise, "and that's how you got hurt."

"It's not your fault," he assured her. "I'm just glad you changed your mind about going there. You made the right choice, Skylar."

She smiled. "You're really not mad at me?"

"Not at all," he said. "I'm proud of you."

Her smile widened and she stepped forward, her arms reaching out for a hug. But then someone rapped on the door frame and Todd, one of the kids who'd just left the group, said, "Hey, Rev, that TV cop's here with some chick cop."

His pulse tripped as it sped up. "Chick cop? What does she look like?"

"Hot! Really hot!" Todd exclaimed. "But kind of uptight, too."

Roberta. Now his pulse raced. He hurried out of the meeting room with Todd and Skylar close behind him. "You know her?" Todd asked, but he didn't wait for an answer. As Holden neared the police officers, the kids slunk off toward the lounge.

"Hey, Rev," Sergeant Kent Terlecki called out as Holden joined them in the main-floor reception area of the four-story building. The tall, golden-haired officer shook Holden's hand and said, "Hope you don't mind us stopping in."

"Not at all," he assured the public-information

officer. Then he met Roberta's blue-eyed gaze and added, "In fact, I appreciate it."

"When Robbie mentioned she was going to check out the shelter, I thought I'd come along," Terlecki explained, "in case you were too busy to show her around. I can give her the grand tour."

Irritation tempered Holden's pleasure at her visit. It wasn't that he didn't like the public-information officer, but he would have liked him more had he not tagged along with Roberta.

"So don't let us get in your way," the sergeant told him, his hand settling with familiarity on the small of Roberta's back.

Holden's irritation grew. "I'm not too busy," he nearly snapped.

Kent glanced from him to Roberta. "If you're sure you have the time."

"I'd be happy…" With his peripheral vision, he noticed that someone else was walking up to join them.

The long-legged brunette closed the distance quickly, despite stopping occasionally to greet some of the kids who hung out watching the wide-screen television. "Meredith…"

She leaned close and kissed his uninjured cheek. "Hi, Holden. I brought lunch." She patted the handle of the picnic basket that hung from one arm.

"Lunch?" he repeated, totally blank on why she'd shown up.

She chuckled. "You invited me, remember?"

"Of course." He nodded as he remembered his late-night revelation and subsequent phone call. "Meredith Wallingford, this is—"

"Sergeant Kent Terlecki and Officer Roberta Meyers," she finished for him with a wide smile as she held out her free hand to shake theirs. "We've met."

"She's our favorite social worker," Kent claimed, showing his notorious charm as he squeezed her hand.

Roberta only nodded, but it wasn't clear if she agreed with the sergeant or was only acknowledging Meredith's greeting.

"Merry's my favorite, too," Holden said. Even though she hadn't conducted the interview that had awarded him custody of Holly, Meredith had given him a glowing letter of recommendation.

"You're making me blush," Meredith protested with a chuckle. "But don't let that stop you from singing my praises."

Kent flashed his patented TV-cop grin. "Just don't you stop. I don't know what Lakewood PD would do without you."

Kent's flirting with his date didn't bother Holden in the least. He'd like to believe it was because he'd known Meredith for so long that he was sure he could trust her.

"You're a sweet talker, Sergeant," Meredith said as color flushed her face. "I don't know why that reporter from the *Chronicle* gives you such a hard time."

Kent's grin slipped. "You and me both, Meredith."

Holden ignored the two of them and focused again on Roberta. She was likewise ignoring the banter between the sergeant and Merry as she stared at him. Or glared, rather. He didn't blame her for being mad at him, though. He wasn't too happy with himself, either; he should have told her that he was seeing someone, however casually.

Finally she spoke. "Sergeant Terlecki can show me around." Her lips lifted in a smile even though her eyes were cold. "Don't let us keep you from your lunch date."

WHAT A FOOL I've been...

When would she ever learn that she couldn't trust her judgment when it came to men? And it wasn't just the men she was interested in she misjudged.

"Thanks," she murmured to Kent Terlecki as they headed up the double stairwell to the second floor.

He paused midstep and turned back to her, his brow furrowed. "For what?"

She forced a smile and said, "Thanks for the tour." Earlier that morning she'd actually resented him for tagging along; she'd thought herself a fool for stopping off at the department to change into her uniform before visiting the shelter. If she'd come alone, she probably would have been in the middle of asking Holden to the ball at the mayor's mansion when his girlfriend walked in with their romantic picnic lunch.

When once just remembering their kiss had made her lips tingle, now they burned as she pressed them together hard, fighting the urge to blast him for cheating on a nice woman like Meredith Wallingford. Kent hadn't been just flirting when he'd claimed she was the department's favorite social worker. Meredith had already had one cheating ex; she deserved better this time. Of course maybe Holden didn't consider a kiss to be cheating. But Roberta did.

"You okay?" Kent asked, his eyes narrowed as he studied her face. "Is it hard for you to be here?"

Heat rushed to her face. Had he picked up on her attraction to the youth minister?

"What do you mean?"

He lifted his broad shoulders in a slight shrug. "Nothing."

"Ah," she said as realization dawned. "You know about my past." Her life wasn't quite the open book she'd told Holden it was. But then she wasn't the only one who hadn't been entirely forthcoming.

"The chief and I are close," he reminded her.

"Yeah, since you took a bullet for him," she said, revealing the fact that she knew the department secret. Kent had been shot three years ago, and Robbie had only been with Lakewood PD for two and a half years. Because the force preferred its officers to have some experience, she'd initially been a county deputy for a couple of years after graduating from the Police Academy at Lakewood University.

Kent grimaced and cursed his roommate. "Damn Billy's big mouth."

Robbie smiled at the embarrassed look on his face and teased, "Brownnoser. Some people will do anything to get ahead."

He sighed. "Yeah, that's what Erin Powell thinks." Erin Powell being the reporter at the *Chronicle* who routinely harassed him.

"She's an idiot. You're a great guy," Robbie said, reaching out to squeeze his arm. "A real hero."

Someone cleared his throat, then remarked, "I hate to interrupt…"

Robbie glanced around to where Holden stood a few steps below them, staring up.

"Now this guy—he's the real hero," Kent said, obviously eager to get the focus off himself.

"No hero here," Holden protested.

Robbie heartily agreed, but before she could voice the comment Kent's phone rang. He glanced at the ID screen. "Excuse me, guys, I gotta take this."

Guys. Most of the male officers on the force saw her that way, one of the guys. She'd thought, after Holden kissed her, that he might have seen her as something else. Well, he did; he saw her as some men had once they'd realized she was a single mother. *Easy.*

"Don't let us interrupt your date with Meredith," she told him.

"I'd like to be the one to show you around the shelter," he said.

"That's not necessary."

"Actually, it is," Kent said as he stepped back onto the landing with them, "if you want to see the place today. I have to go, Rob. There's been an accident, and I need to make a statement to the press."

"Fatalities?" she asked. The accident had to be severe if he needed to make a press release about it; otherwise he'd be on the news every five minutes about one fender bender or another.

He nodded. "I'll send someone back to pick you up when you're done."

"No," she said, "I can leave now, with you."

Kent shook his head. "It's important that you tour the place."

He knew how much she would've liked having someplace like this to go to when she'd been a runaway. "Okay."

Holden waited until Kent had rushed off before speaking again. "I'm glad you decided to stay."

"You don't need to babysit me," she assured him. "I can check the place out by myself. And you can go back to Meredith."

"She left."

"I'm sorry."

"No, you're not. You're pissed."

"Not at all," she lied. She wasn't mad at him; she was mad at herself for being foolish enough to consider dating him.

"You should be mad at me," he said, then lowered his voice to a whisper and added, "I shouldn't have kissed you that night."

"No, you shouldn't have," she agreed. "But it was just a kiss." A kiss she'd thought about much too often. "And it's forgotten."

He nodded his acceptance of her claim. Maybe the kiss hadn't meant anything but a thank-you to her for saving him from being shot at the warehouse. He wasn't really attracted to her. Then he said, "*I* want to show you around."

She lifted a brow in question.

"I want to introduce you to the kids," he explained. "I think it's important that they meet you."

She snorted. "Is that why they slink away every time I so much as glance at them?"

How many of these kids had outstanding warrants? She'd bet quite a few—probably more than the youth minister suspected. Or didn't he even suspect? Was he so idealistic that he had no idea how many of these kids had been in trouble? While some might have been running away from bad home situations, some ran because they'd gotten in trouble with the law, and they couldn't go home because that was the first place the police would look for them. Perhaps he hadn't thought through all the consequences of his request for officers to visit the shelter.

"So can we skip the upstairs?" she asked, seeing that most of the kids were either in the main-floor lounge or heading to the dining room for lunch. And the less time she spent with Holden, the better.

"I can show the upper floors to you later, but the second floor has rooms for teenage mothers and their children. Third is just girls. Fourth, just boys."

"And you have chaperones who keep the boys and girls apart?"

"Each floor has a chaperone," he said.

"What about a security guard?" Often these run-aways were in the most danger from their fellow runaways, kids who'd do *anything* to survive. Or they were kids who'd wound up on the streets because of what they'd already done.

"The shelter has security."

She leaned over the stairwell and peered across the foyer to the main lounge. She saw an older man leaning against the wall watching television, not the kids. "Him?"

"He's a retired cop."

"When did he retire?" she asked. "During the Carter administration?" She turned her attention from the security guard to a particular kid who was obviously trying to disappear into the shadows. But the windows were tall and sunlight poured through them, shining on a face she'd never forget. He wasn't fast enough to escape her. *Not this time.* She vaulted over the stairwell and charged after him.

Holden was stunned. One minute she was ahead of him on the stairs and the next she was gone, leaving behind only a flurry of curses. He rushed after her, pushing past the kids milling about in the wake of the running police officer. Pots, pans and metal racks rattled as Holden slammed through the swinging doors into the kitchen.

The back door stood open, sun blazing down on the cooks who'd gathered in the doorway. Holden shoved between them and scrambled into the alley.

Grunts and groans drew his attention to the other side of a Dumpster. He raced over to find the kid, a burly youngster, lying atop Roberta, his big hands gripping her throat, choking her. Holden, shaking with fear and rage, reached for him, but suddenly the kid convulsed and flipped onto his back. His convulsions continued, sending him across the asphalt like a drop of oil on a hot griddle. Two wire leads traveled from his side to the Taser Roberta held. Coughing and choking, she propped herself up on an elbow.

He dropped to his knees beside her. "Are you okay?"

She shook her head and fumbled her cell from her belt. "C-c-call 911," she rasped.

KAYLA CRAWLED into Aunt JoJo's closet. With the cordless phone pinched between her jaw and shoulder, she pulled shut the folding doors. Light from the hall shone through the slats, so that it wasn't totally dark. But she wasn't scared of the dark, anyway. It was the squealing coming from the phone that had her nerves on edge.

"Shh," she cautioned her friend. "Don't get too excited."

"But your mom went to visit Uncle Holden's shelter," Holly said. "That must mean she likes him."

"That'd be cool," Kayla admitted, smiling. She liked her friend's idea of them being sisters, of all of them being a family. She liked it a lot.

"It'd be the best!"

Kayla sighed, hating that she had to be the serious one, but she needed to point out, "Mom could just be there for work, though." She crinkled her forehead as she remembered. "She wasn't supposed to work today. She told me she'd pick me up from school, but then Aunt JoJo picked me up, instead. And now she's still not home."

"My uncle's not home, either. They gotta be together. This is really great!" Holly squealed again.

Kayla pulled the phone away from her ear so she wouldn't go deaf. Then she gasped as the closet doors rattled. Through the slats she spied Sassy, the dog's tiny front paws, one black like the rest of her and the other white like the patch on her chest, pushing against the wood until the doors folded open. Then she jumped onto Kayla's lap, yipping and licking.

Dodging the little dog's black-spotted tongue, Kayla squirmed from beneath the coats hanging over her head.

"There you are," Aunt JoJo said from the hall, "I had to release the hound to find you. And this apartment is pretty darn small. I didn't know we were playing hide-and-seek."

Kayla laughed. "I'm not hiding. I had to call Holly."

She lifted the phone to her ear and then added the explanation her friend had whispered through the receiver, "about homework."

"You're doing homework in here?" Joelly lifted the sleeve of a coat and rattled the hangers. "Not much light." She narrowed her eyes. "And where are your books?"

"I…I…"

Joelly laughed. "Don't worry. It's okay to just want to talk to your friend."

"Best friend."

"Sisters soon!" Holly yelled through the phone.

"Shh…bye!" Kayla clicked off the phone and handed it back to Jo. "You didn't hear that?"

Aunt JoJo shook her head, but a smile tugged at her lips. "I didn't hear a thing." She turned away, heading back down the hall to the living room. "I'm way ahead of you, kiddo."

"What?" Kayla asked, scrambling after her.

"On the video game," she explained. "I got my bubble rolled farther through the canyon."

"Did you get to the rainbow?"

"Not yet."

That was like Holly wanting them to become sisters. They weren't there yet, and a lot of things could pop their bubble before they were.

Chapter Six

An icepack wrapped around her neck, Robbie settled back on the couch and picked up the fleece throw she'd dropped when she answered the door moments earlier. She'd no more than folded her legs beneath her when another knock rattled the wood.

Despite her swollen throat, she managed a sigh and lurched to her feet again. Her legs trembled with leftover adrenaline as she stumbled down the short hall.

"Jo, I'm fine," she said as she turned the doorknob. "You don't need to keep mothering me."

But it was not her best friend standing in the hall between their apartments. "Oh..." She gripped the edge of the door and was tempted to slam it in Holden's handsome, cheating face. "What are you doing here?"

He gestured at her throat. "I had to check on you," he said, his voice gruff with emotion. "I had to make sure you were really okay."

"Like I told you in the alley, I'm fine," she replied. Of course she hadn't been able to utter those words right away; it had taken her a while to find her voice again. "You should be home…with your niece. I wouldn't want to make you late again."

"Mrs. Crayden is with her, and Holly's sleeping. I assume Kayla is, too, since they have school in the morning." He shifted his gaze to the door she held tight. "Is that why you won't let me in?"

"It is," she said. "Partly."

"You're really mad at me," he said, "about the kiss."

"I'm not mad about the kiss. I told you, it's forgotten." Maybe if she made that claim enough times, she'd begin to believe it. But her gaze was drawn to his mouth, to his lips.

"Yeah, you said that, and then you jumped off the stairs and ran one of my kids out of the shelter."

"Your kid?" She snorted. "Your kid is actually twenty-three and wanted for assault."

He sucked in a breath. "Twenty-three?"

"No one told you?"

"The police officers who responded to your 911 call didn't talk to me. They wouldn't tell me what was going on."

Robbie closed her eyes, her head pounding as she remembered the chaos in the alley. Kent Terlecki might never forgive himself for leaving her alone at the shelter, no matter how much she assured him she was fine. "I was actually talking about one of your other kids, not the police officers. None of them told you the truth about him?"

He shook his head. "The ones who stuck around stayed real quiet."

He probably blamed her for that. So she'd been right; more had outstanding warrants than just the perp she'd caught. "It was your idea that I visit the shelter," she reminded him. "I bet you regret that now."

"The only thing I regret is your getting hurt," he said, his eyes warm with sincerity. "Please, tell me what happened."

She was probably too keyed up to sleep yet, anyway. So she pushed the door wide open. "You might as well come in."

He hesitated. "I don't want to wake Kayla."

"You're more likely to wake her if we keep talking out here in the hall," she said. "She's at my neighbor's. She fell asleep over there, and I didn't want to wake her." She shifted the ice pack against her neck, hoping the swelling would be down by morning and the bruises light enough that she could cover them with makeup.

"You don't want her to see you like this," he surmised as he stepped into the apartment. He stood close, his gaze intent on her face. "I can see now that it's been broken."

"What?"

"Your nose."

She touched a finger to it, then shrugged. "It adds character."

"Is that what Kayla thought when she saw it?"

She shut the door, knowing that her voice, despite the swelling, would probably get louder. "Are you criticizing my parenting again?"

He shook his head. "I just don't understand it. I don't understand why a single mother would put herself in danger, like the way you ran after that kid— that guy—today."

She flinched, having already realized back in the alley that that hadn't been her smartest move. "I was working a couple months ago when he assaulted an elderly woman and stole her purse." She'd been a vice decoy that night and hadn't been able to chase him, and her backup officer hadn't managed to catch him, either. "I wasn't going to let him get away again."

"Even though he almost killed you?" Holden asked, his face pale with concern.

Robbie managed a laugh. "He didn't almost kill me." Although she *had* been closer to blacking out than she was comfortable remembering. "I had it under control."

Now, if only she could control her attraction to Holden. Even now, knowing he was involved with a woman she admired, she couldn't help noticing how his thin sweater molded itself to the sculpted muscles of his chest.

Holden reached for her and gently shifted the ice pack. As he studied her swollen neck, he grimaced, and with his voice shaking, he argued, "You didn't have anything under control. Why…why do you put yourself in danger like that?"

"Because it's my job." She couldn't express exactly what that job meant to her. It didn't mean everything— because *Kayla* was everything. But close.

"You need a new job."

First she drew in a breath of surprise, and then she laughed. "Wow, you have some nerve, Reverend. How would you feel if I told you to close the shelter?"

The corners of his mouth lifted in a slight grin. "That would make no sense. Why would you say that?"

"Because it's dangerous."

"The shelter?"

She gestured toward her neck.

"But that was because of you," he said, "because you—"

"Because I arrested an assault suspect? Should I have let him get away? I thought you were running a shelter, not a sanctuary for criminals."

Her accusation gave Holden pause. He *had* intended the shelter to be a sanctuary—but for kids who needed protection, like Lorielle. His head pounded, and he raised a hand to massage his forehead. "I…that isn't…"

"You know what we found on him?" she asked, not giving Holden time to answer. "A bag of crack—a substantial amount that had to be for more than personal use. He was selling."

"At the shelter?" His stomach pitched. If he'd actually eaten anything since breakfast, he might have thrown up. "God, no. Not drugs."

The ice pack dropped to the floor, making a thud as it struck the hardwood. Then Robbie reached for him, her small hands touching his arms. "Holden? Are you all right?"

He shook his head. "It's just… It goes against everything I started the shelter for."

Her voice barely a whisper, she asked, "Why *did* you start the shelter?"

He released a ragged sigh. "For my sister. Holly's mother. Lorielle was a teen runaway."

"That must have been hard on you and your parents."

Bitterness filled him. "I think they were relieved."

She slid her arms around his waist. But he wondered whom she was comforting, him or herself, when she added, "My parents were relieved when I ran away."

"You were a runaway," he stated, his suspicions confirmed. He'd been right; she *was* the officer with whom the kids could most relate.

"Yeah, you didn't make a mistake at the warehouse. You were just nine years late with your assessment," she said with a hoarse chuckle.

"Why…how? What's your story, Roberta?" He really wanted to know.

She shrugged. "Nothing extraordinary. Like I already said, my parents weren't thrilled when I got pregnant. They wanted me to get rid of…*it.*" Pain flashed in her eyes, and Holden suspected it had nothing to do with her injury and everything to do with her memories. "I wanted to keep her, so I ran away."

"You were pregnant when you ran away?"

"Pregnant and fifteen," she said dismissively, as if what she'd endured—the fear and pain of running away—had been nothing. "That's my story. Now tell me about Lorielle."

"Robbie—"

She clutched his sweater, her fingers trembling. "I want to hear about Lorielle."

He blew out a ragged breath. "My mom definitely was relieved when she ran away, even though Lorielle didn't live with us. My half sister reminded my mother of my father's midlife crisis, when he left her for a younger woman. He was only married to Lorielle's mom for a few years before he came to his senses, as my mother says. I tried to keep in touch with Lorielle…" But it had been so hard, with his mother acting as if his love for his younger sister was a betrayal.

"You were just a kid, too," she said, defending him.

"A selfish, self-centered kid," he admitted. "I kept

busy with my friends and with school. And I didn't talk to or see Lorielle as much as I should have. I should have kept in better touch with her. I should have known how unhappy she was."

"How long did she live on the streets?" Roberta asked.

"She'd been gone a year before I found her, alone and pregnant and suffering major withdrawal. For her unborn child—Holly. She stayed clean until she had her. Then she'd drop Holly off with me and go back to the streets for drugs. I kept trying to get her to stick with rehab, but she'd swear she was better and leave early. And she would stay clean—for a while, just long enough to fool me into thinking that it had worked. But she couldn't stay off the streets or off the drugs, no matter how much she loved her daughter. And I believe she *did* love her but…"

"She was an addict," Robbie said with complete understanding.

How could she understand something *he* still struggled to accept?

"Were you?" he asked.

She shook her head. "No, but I've met a lot of addicts. It's not easy for them, no matter how much they might want to quit."

"Every time she took off, I worried that she wouldn't come back. I'd track her down, and the way I'd find her, beaten up…" His breath shuddered out, and he clutched Roberta close, needing her warmth and softness as the memory of his loss tore him apart. "I started the shelter so that kids like Lorielle would have a safe place to stay."

Robbie's arms tightened. "You can make it work," she assured him. "You just need better security. A metal detector at the door and security guards who actually pay attention to what's going on."

"But won't that scare the kids away?"

"Only kids like the twenty-three-year-old dealer. The ones who really need you and want your help will come," she promised him.

"Why don't you come to the shelter?" he asked.

She laughed. "I'm not a runaway anymore. And especially after today, it's probably a good idea if I stay away."

"No, you should quit the department and come to work there," he urged her, the idea filling him with hope. "You could head security." Not only could she help him make the shelter safer, she would stay safe herself.

"Holden, why would you ask me that?"

"I can't handle what you do for a living," he admitted. "I hadn't gone out with Merry in months. But after watching those videos of you putting yourself in danger over and over again, I called her."

"So you're not seriously dating?" she asked.

He shook his head. "We've known each other for years, grew up together…"

"High-school sweethearts?"

"Friends. *Only* friends." Even now, that was really all they were. All they might ever be because of Robbie.

His hands shook when he cupped her face in his palms, tipping it up to his. He slid his thumb across her mouth. Her lips were so silky—he had to feel them with his.

He lowered his head and kissed her, bracing himself for her reaction—possibly shoving him away, slapping him or even kneeing him in the groin. He wasn't prepared for her to kiss him back, however. The force of her passion, as her mouth moved beneath his and her fingers tangled in his hair, staggered him.

Her lips parted, and he slid his tongue across her full bottom lip into the moist heat of her mouth. He groaned. And she moaned, pressing against him and spiking his desire for her. Despite her petite size, the woman had curves. He smoothed his hands down her back to her hips, pulling her tight against his straining erection.

She dragged her mouth from beneath his and pushed against his chest. Panting for breath, she asked, "Are you sure you and Meredith are just friends?"

He nodded.

She arched into him, rubbing against his hips.

He leaned forward and kissed her again, just brushing his lips across hers. Then he slid his tongue into her mouth, tasting the sweetness. He wanted to taste her everywhere. He moved his hands, sliding them up from her waist over her ribs to cup her breasts. Despite the thick cotton of her sweatshirt, her nipples pressed into his palms. She wore no bra. His body tensed with desire to the point of pain. "Roberta…"

She arched into his hands and murmured his name.

"What are we doing?" he asked.

Robbie shook her head, unable to think. She could only feel. She held him tightly, her hands grasping his sweater and her fingers pressing the hard muscles beneath the soft wool.

He kissed her again, his tongue sliding in and out of her mouth, mimicking the action her body craved. His hand moved again, to the hem of her sweatshirt, and he eased up the material.

Robbie tensed and shoved her palms against his

chest—not because she had finally come to her senses but because the apartment door opened.

"What…?" Holden murmured, obviously confused. He reached for her again.

But she pushed him away and focused on her daughter, who stood in the doorway. Kayla rubbed her hands over her eyes as if unable to believe what she was seeing.

"Sw-sweetheart," Robbie said. "I was going to come and get you."

"M-mom?" Kayla asked, her voice thick with sleep.

Perhaps she was too groggy to realize what she'd caught her mother doing—and with whom. Robbie reached for her, closing her hands around Kayla's shoulders to steer the sleepy child toward her bedroom. Before Kayla stumbled through the doorway, she turned back to Holden, standing in the hall. "Good night, Mr. Thomas."

He cleared his throat before replying, "Good night, honey."

Robbie helped Kayla into bed and pulled the covers to her chin. The child's eyes closed, as if her lids were too heavy to hold open. Hopefully she hadn't seen anything—either her mother making out with Holly's uncle or the swelling on her neck.

Robbie kissed her daughter's forehead. She'd thought of Kayla when the assailant's hands closed around her neck. Kayla was why she'd fought back using the stun gun. She would do whatever was necessary to come home to her daughter.

With one last glance at her sleeping child, she straightened and braced herself to return to her visitor.

"She's sleeping?" Holden asked. His eyes darkened, the pupils dilating with desire.

Robbie nodded, but she stepped back when Holden reached for her. "We can't. We shouldn't have—"

"We're both adults here, Roberta. We *can*."

She shook her head. "I forgot myself for a moment." And if Kayla hadn't walked in, something might have happened between them. Hell, it definitely would have happened. Even now Robbie's breasts ached for his touch, the pressure so tight inside her that she hurt. "But Kayla's home now. I wouldn't want you accusing me of being a bad mother again."

"I shouldn't have said that you put your job before her."

He had only voiced her greatest fear aloud. "You shouldn't have thought it, either."

"I thought I was wrong," he admitted, "until I saw those videos the other night. And then today…" His voice trailed off, as if he was the one being choked.

"That's my job, just my job." Robbie gestured toward Kayla's closed bedroom door. "She's my life."

"Then quit the department and take the job I offered you at the shelter. It's well funded. I can probably afford to pay you more than the Lakewood PD does." He gestured toward Kayla's bedroom. "Do it for her."

This was one of the reasons she'd chosen to stay un-involved. Inevitably, if a man claimed to care about you, he wanted to tell you what to do or *not* do.

"I'm a police officer *for her*," she said, then she tried to explain. "I am a police officer to make the city safer for her. I'm a police officer so that her mother is someone she can admire."

"I admire you," he said, "but I can't…be with you."

A twinge of disappointment struck her heart, but she

forced a humorless chuckle. "I don't remember proposing to you."

"Roberta…"

"Robbie," she corrected him.

"You probably think I'm a chauvinist, wanting you
to quit your job."

"I know you're not," she assured him. "You just
don't want to get involved with a cop." She'd heard
some fellow officers commiserating over that problem. Women either wanted to be with them because
they were cops or didn't want to be with them for the
same reason.

"I can't…" He gripped his temples again, as if his
head was pounding. "Holly and I lived with so much uncertainty because of her mother. When she'd go out to
score drugs Lorielle constantly put herself in danger."

"I don't…" Then she remembered that she did, that
she had as a vice decoy. "I don't know what to say."

"I couldn't put Holly through that uncertainty
again—getting attached to you only to lose you like she
did her mother." His throat moved as he swallowed
hard. "I can't put myself through that again, either. I
can't care about you."

She flinched, the disappointment greater than a
twinge now. She was afraid it was too late for her; she
already cared about him. "If that's how you feel…"

"It's not just about me."

"Holly." Robbie got it. The poor kid had already
been through enough in her young life.

"It's about Lorielle, too," Holden said. "You've
probably realized…she died from a drug overdose."

"I'm sorry." She held out her arms to offer him

comfort again, but he stepped back and shoved his hands into his pockets.

"She was still conscious when I found her."

He had been there. Robbie's heart ached with the pain he must have endured.

"And she asked me for one last promise. She wanted me to take care of Holly," he said.

"Of course. She gave you custody."

"She wanted more for Holly than just me. She wanted me to find her a mother, to give her the family that Lorielle only had for those first few years—" his voice grew rough with bitterness "—before my father came to his senses."

"Holden…"

"She made me promise to give her daughter the loving family and secure home she wished she'd had for herself." He closed his eyes. "If she'd had that love and security, she would still be alive. She wouldn't have run away."

"You can't blame yourself for any of that," Robbie said. "It wasn't your fault your parents got back together."

"No," he agreed. "But I was happy that they did. I was happy that I got *my* loving, secure home back. But it came at a great cost. It cost me my sister."

Tears of sympathy stung her eyes. "Holden, you can't keep all this guilt. You have to let it go."

He shook his head. "No, it reminds me of how I failed Lorielle. It reminds me that I can't do that again. I need to fulfill my promise to her."

"And you can't do that with me."

He shook his head.

"Then I guess you'd better become more than just

friends with Meredith," she suggested, even though the thought of it brought her more pain than having her windpipe nearly crushed. "She'd be perfect for you. And Holly."

"But whenever I'm near you…" He held out his hand again, this time curling his fingers into his palm before he actually touched her.

She drew a shaky breath. "Then I guess we shouldn't be near each other."

He nodded. "We need to stay away from each other."

"Yes," she agreed and she opened the door for him. "That would be best." For Holden and Holly, and for her.

She could not lose her heart to a man who wouldn't be able to love her as she was, who would only love her if she did what he wanted. She had lost her parents' love because she'd defied them, and she would not be manipulated or controlled that way again. She would only love someone who could love her unconditionally.

And that man was not Holden Thomas—no matter how much she wished he was.

Chapter Seven

Maybe she would have to take Holden's job offer, after all. Robbie's finger shook as she pushed the elevator button for the second floor of the police station. First thing this morning one of the interns who staffed the front desk had called and summoned her to a meeting with the chief.

How pissed would he be about her scuffle at the shelter? Not pissed enough to fire her, she hoped. The bell dinged as the elevator car lurched to a stop. She filled her lungs with air, hoping to calm her racing pulse. Then the doors slid open to…him. And her breath disappeared in a rush.

"So much for staying away from each other," Holden said with a tentative smile that didn't reach his eyes. Dark circles underlined the green-blue orbs.

He hadn't slept any better than she had. Perversely, that gave her a small measure of satisfaction. "What are you doing here?" she asked.

"Giving another statement."

"To the chief?"

"Lieutenant O'Donnell's in there with Chief Archer and Sergeant Terlecki."

This is worse than I thought. She had to face three superiors at once. It felt like a firing squad.

Holden shrugged, then his shoulders sagged as if under an enormous burden. "I don't know why they bothered taking a statement from me. I never know what's going on."

As she stepped out of the elevator, her arm brushed his. She wanted to do more; she wanted to give him another hug of support. "Don't beat yourself up about yesterday. You've helped a lot of kids."

"And apparently a few I shouldn't have helped."

"You can't always know."

"I'm going to work on that," he said, "making the changes you suggested."

"I'm sorry," she said. "I know metal detectors and security guards aren't how you envisioned the place."

He sighed. "No, they aren't."

Worrying over those changes was no doubt what had kept him awake last night, not their decision to stay away from each other. A decision neither seemed eager to honor at the moment. Robbie told herself it was just because she was putting off stepping in front of that firing squad. It wasn't because she was unable to walk away from Holden—even standing a foot apart from him, she felt connected. And she didn't want to sever that connection.

Holden appeared equally reluctant, his gaze intent on her face, his eyes turbulent with mixed emotions. "Why are you here?" he asked. "I thought you'd be resting this morning."

She touched her fingertips to the pink scarf she'd wrapped around her neck. Thankfully, scarves had become a fashion statement lately. "I'm fine."

"Did Kayla notice?" he asked with concern.

She shook her head, her lips curving in a small smile. "She was happy I'm wearing this. She gave it to me for Valentine's Day this year."

"She has good taste," he said. "It's pretty." But his gaze was focused on her face, as if the appreciative gleam in his eyes was for her.

She ignored the flip of her stomach. She couldn't let herself be drawn back into this futile attraction, not when she knew he would never be able to accept her. "I have to go." She glanced toward the hall leading to the chief's office. "I don't want to be late."

He nodded and stepped inside the waiting elevator. "I understand. Goodbye, Roberta."

She waited until the doors closed, hiding him from her sight before she managed to respond. "Goodbye."

"Hey, Rob," a deep voice called out. "You're here."

She turned and saw the watch commander leaning against the wall outside the chief's office. Paddy O'Donnell's perceptiveness was legendary in Lakewood; the man missed nothing. What had he seen of her exchange with Holden Thomas?

She squared her shoulders, refusing to let thoughts of the man distract her any longer. She closed the short distance between the elevator and the chief's office. "Yes, I'm here."

"We thought maybe you changed your mind about coming in so early."

Changed her mind? "I didn't realize I had a choice."

"The intern didn't let you pick the time that was most convenient for you?"

Maybe he had. Robbie had only heard his first words,

"The chief wants to see you." She shrugged. "This is fine. I was up anyway to get Kayla off to school."

"Come in," he invited, stepping back so she could pass through the doorway.

The chief sat behind his desk. Kent Terlecki stood next to him, in front of the windows that overlooked the city, with the lake in the distance. They both turned at her entrance. The chief scanned her face and eyed the scarf that covered her neck.

O'Donnell offered an explanation for her delayed arrival. "She ran into the reverend by the elevator."

Chief Archer planted his palms on his desk, rose from his chair and uttered a profound sigh of relief. "Thank God you're all right, Roberta."

She suppressed her own sigh of relief. He wouldn't be so happy to see her if he was going to fire her. Right?

But before she could completely relax, he pointed a finger and admonished her, "You're damn lucky you're alive after that crazy stunt you pulled."

The chief was a big man, closer to seven feet tall than six, with a bellow that could rattle windows. Roberta locked her knees so that she wouldn't cower or grovel for forgiveness. She just nodded. "You're right."

"It's my fault," Kent said as he pulled out a chair for Robbie. "I shouldn't have left her there."

"You had to," she reminded him. "*I* didn't have to run after that kid on my own."

"Yes, you did." The chief chuckled and settled back into his chair. "I've known you a long time, Roberta Meyers. *You* did. You couldn't let him go. It's not in you to let an assailant get away."

She dropped into the chair. "I wish I had that kind

of control," she admitted, "but we all know that more of them get away than we'd like."

"If one gets away, it's too many," the chief said.

The other two men nodded in agreement. Archer addressed them. "Hey, guys, I'd like to talk to Officer Meyers alone."

"Sure," Kent said, and he paused beside Robbie's chair and squeezed her shoulder. "I really am sorry."

She patted his hand. "You have nothing to be sorry about. But thanks."

"Rob," Paddy said, "I won't be seeing you at roll call, so take care of yourself."

Before she could ask the watch commander what he meant—and why the heck she wouldn't be at roll call—he and Kent headed out the door. She waited, but the chief said nothing. He just leaned back in his chair and studied her, his brow furrowed.

After a few long moments Robbie reminded him, "You wanted to *talk* to me, which usually implies that you're going to say something."

He chuckled at her sassiness. "I was just thinking…"

"About what?"

"About the first time I saw you."

Heat rushed to her face. "I wish you would forget about that."

The chief grinned, the skin around his pale blue eyes crinkling at the corners. Salt wound through the black pepper of his thick, short hair, but he wasn't all that old—just old enough to be her father. If only he had been.

"I can't," he said, shaking his head. "That image haunts me—how I found you and Joelly Standish in that dark alley…" He shuddered. "That's what I thought of when I heard what happened yesterday, because then, too, you could have been killed."

"I'm fine."

"No, you're not," he said, his voice edging closer to the bellow he sometimes used for effect. "You can sell this tough act to everyone else, but not me. I've known you too long, girl."

Her lips twitched in a smile. "You knew me at my worst."

"Desperate and scared to death," he remembered. "I still glimpse that girl sometimes, when you drop the wall you've built around yourself."

Tears stung Robbie's eyes, but she blinked them back. "You *have* known me too long." She forced a smile. "And too well…"

"That's how I know you're not fine," he said, pointing his finger at her again. "And that's why you're going to take a few days off."

"You're suspending me?" It was better than straight out being fired, but not much. "Am I in trouble for using excessive force?"

The chief snorted. "You should have shot the little bastard. It would have been justified." His voice trembled as he added, "He could have killed you."

"I'm—"

"Don't!" he warned, shaking his finger at her. "Don't lie to me, Roberta. Not again."

Heat, hotter this time, rushed to her face. "You knew…"

"That you were the one trying to sell the drugs?" He nodded. "Yeah, I knew."

"But I let Joelly take the blame." And even though

nearly ten years had passed, it still nagged at Roberta that she'd been such a coward. But Joelly had convinced her that the authorities would take away her baby the minute it was born if she had a record.

"She insisted," Chief Archer reminded her. "And we both know there's no talking that little girl out of whatever she sets her mind to."

Robbie laughed. "Ain't that the truth. You think her father will ever figure that out?"

Frank Archer shook his head. "Joel Standish? He'd have to think about someone other than himself for once."

"He's not that bad," Robbie said in his defense. "He took me in when my own parents wouldn't let me come home." The chief had called them; she suspected he'd even made a personal visit to argue on her behalf. But because it had been too late for her to get an abortion, they hadn't wanted her back. She shrugged off the pain—she'd made peace with the fact that she had no relationship with her parents.

And she refused to think about the other relationship she was being denied, the one with the man who didn't want her as she was. Instead, she forced her mind back to the mayor and laughed. "Of course, Joelly didn't give him much choice. She swore she'd run away again if he didn't let me come live with them."

Regret filled the chief's eyes. "I'm sorry."

"Sorry because no one wanted me?" She shrugged. "I'm used to it." But she couldn't deny that it still hurt like hell.

"No. Sorry because I didn't bring you to live with me and my wife," Frank Archer said. "I wanted to."

"That's sweet," she said, "but you don't have to say that. It was a long time ago. I'm over it."

"I'm not. I regret, every day, that we didn't foster you. But my wife had gotten sick…" He flinched as if the pain of her loss was physical. "She still wanted us to become foster parents, but we wouldn't have gotten approved—not with her cancer." He sighed. "She beat it, though. That time…"

Seeing how much pain he was still in over the loss of his wife made Robbie think it was better, safer, never to fall in love.

"Go home," the chief told her.

She suspected that at the moment he just wanted to be alone. "I can't miss any of my shifts," she said. "We're already short-staffed."

"Is that why you agreed to work the vice unit?"

She nodded. "And because I'm best suited to it."

"You're a very effective decoy," he responded. "Reverend Thomas would even swear to that."

"You need me out there," she said.

"I need you one hundred percent." He gestured toward her throat. "While the scarf's pretty, it can't hide the fact that you're hurt. You need to take it easy. No argument."

"It's just that I feel guilty taking time off when everyone else is working doubles."

His jaw clenched in frustration. "I have to talk some sense into the city council. I need more officers."

"Joelly and I are going to work on her dad at his ball."

"If anyone can get through to him, it's his daughter." He stood up and came around his desk. "So what's it going to take to get through to you?"

She sighed and rose to her feet. "I'll follow your orders." She smiled. "I was a wreck about coming down here. I was worried you were going to fire me."

He shook his head. "You know I need you too much." He held up a hand to prevent another argument about taking time off. "But I can spare you for a few days, and I'll be surprised if you manage to stay away that long. This job means too much to you. I could never take it away from you."

While she knew it wasn't very professional, she couldn't hold back and she threw her arms around the chief. At least someone accepted her for who she was.

HOLDEN CLOSED his eyes, forcing Robbie's face from his mind. He had to forget about her. He opened them again and focused on Meredith, sitting across the booth from him at a diner around the corner from her office. "Sorry about yesterday," he said, "about bailing on our picnic."

"I understand," she said with an easy smile. "You had visitors from the police department. It's important to have them involved in the shelter." She reached across the table and patted his hand.

"You heard about what happened?"

She nodded. "I'm sorry."

He fisted his hand. "But he was dealing drugs in my shelter. He never should have been there." He closed his eyes again, and behind his lids flashed the image of those hands around Robbie's throat.

"I've been conned a time or ten. You can't let it get to you. You can't let it change you." Meredith squeezed, then released his fingers. "You're doing so much good."

"I need to do better." He sighed. "At a lot of things.

Not only did I bail on our lunch, but I promised I'd call you for dinner. And I never called."

"You were busy," she excused Holden. "And I'm sure you were concerned about Robbie. How is she?"

"Fine, or so she insists."

Meredith laughed. "That's Robbie for you. You'd never guess from her small size how tough she is."

He touched his fingers to his cheek, where the bruise had faded. "She's tough. But one day she'll take on more than she can handle."

"Don't worry about Robbie," Meredith said softly. "She can take care of herself. She's been doing it for a long time."

"You really know her," he realized with surprise. Meredith was probably only five or six years older than Robbie, and she couldn't have been her social worker back when Robbie had been living on the streets. He wished she had been, because there was still so much he didn't know about Robbie's past, including how she'd gotten off the streets when his sister had never managed to for long. "How do you know her? Just through the police department?"

"Robbie is a social worker's best friend. She goes the extra mile with runaways to make sure we're not returning them to an abusive home." Her brown eyes glowed with admiration. "She has some kind of sixth sense about them. She can figure out which ones have run away just over something stupid, like a strict curfew or a forbidden boyfriend, and which ones had no choice." She tapped her fingers on the table. "You really need her at the shelter."

"She's too busy…with her job and Kayla."

Meredith laughed. "She reminds me of you."

And maybe that was the problem. He and Robbie were too much alike. Holly needed someone who would have more time for her.

"I don't want to talk about Robbie," he said. He didn't even want to think about her. "I want to talk about us."

"Holden—"

"I got an invitation to a ball at the mayor's mansion," he said, shaking his head, still surprised his name had been included on the guest list. "I'd like you to go with me."

She narrowed her eyes and studied him. "Are you sure I'm the woman you want to invite?"

"Wh-what do you mean?"

"I saw the way you and Robbie looked at each other yesterday. Something's going on between you two."

His friend was pretty and smart. If only he was attracted to her the way he was to Roberta Meyers.

He shook his head. "We would never work." Robbie probably thought he was crazy, asking her to quit her job when they hardly knew each other. And because they hardly knew each other, she would be easy to forget. He would forget all about her.

"And you suddenly think, after all these years we've known each other, that *we* will?" Meredith asked with a smile that gently mocked him.

"You think I'm nuts."

"I think you're scared." She sighed. "And after my disastrous marriage and divorce, I certainly don't blame you."

She understood him—maybe better than he understood himself. She was the right woman for him. She had to be.

"I want you to think about this for a bit," she encouraged him, "make sure *I'm* the woman you want to take."

Maybe she understood him too well.

KAYLA'S HEAD bobbed back and forth. "Hey," she murmured in sleepy protest.

Holly nudged her shoulder again. "Wake up. Mrs. Groom is going to yell at you," she warned.

Kayla rubbed a hand over her eyes, wiping the sleep from them. Then she looked at their teacher, with her hair as black and frizzy as a witch's wig. She was standing at the chalkboard in front of the room and she wasn't looking at them. Yet. To keep it that way, Kayla whispered back, "I was up late last night."

"Why? Did you have a bad dream?" Holly's voice quavered as she asked the question—she must have had some really bad dreams of her own. Losing her mother had to have been the worst nightmare ever, but it had been real, not a dream.

Kayla gave Holly a nudge now. "No bad dream," she told her friend. "I was over at Aunt JoJo's apartment and when I came home to sleep in my own bed I found your uncle with my mom."

"So Uncle Holden was with your mom last night. Yes!" Holly squealed, which earned a glare from Mrs. Groom.

Kayla had hoped they were together, but she'd still been surprised when she'd opened the door and found her mom and Mr. Thomas in each other's arms. "Yup, they were together."

"On a date?" Holly asked.

"I don't know. But I walked in on them kissing."

Holly clapped her hands. This time Mrs. Groom yelled her usual warning: "Don't make me separate you two again!"

Kayla had never gotten yelled at before Holly had started coming to her school. She smiled, secretly happy that she wasn't the class mouse anymore. But because she didn't want Mrs. Groom to have a stroke yelling at them again, she waited until the old lady got busy with some other kids before she turned back to her friend.

"They kissed," Holly said, her eyes widening. "And you thought it was going to be hard to get them together."

"It will be hard," Kayla warned the other girl. "I pretended to be asleep, but I listened at my door. They were talking quiet, though, so I didn't hear everything. But they did say something about it never working and that they needed to stay away from each other."

"They're not going to be able to stay away from each other," Holly insisted. "They're going to see each other because Uncle Holden is in the Police Academy."

"Citizens' Police Academy," Kayla automatically corrected her friend. "My mom doesn't have to teach anything for a couple more weeks, though."

"Well, we can't let them go two weeks before they see each other again," Holly said, shaking her head. "I think it's time for another sleepover. This time, my house. And you will have a bad dream."

"What do you mean?"

"We'll think of some way to get your mom back over and get them to kiss again." Holly trembled with excitement. "And then they'll fall in love and get married."

Kayla smiled at her friend's optimism. Holly hadn't overheard the conversation *she* had, though. Her mom and Mr. Thomas seemed pretty determined to stay away from each other. But then she remembered the way they'd been kissing when she walked in—as if they were in some movie about people falling in love—and hope fluttered to life.

Maybe she would have a dream, but not a bad dream. Maybe her dream of having a father would finally come true.

Chapter Eight

Holden wiped his damp palm on his jeans, then wrapped his fingers around the knob and pulled open the door. The tension and anticipation that had gripped him fled, replaced with disappointment.

"Oh…" Holly murmured from behind him, apparently sharing his feelings, despite her friend's arrival. "Hi, Miss Jo."

Was this Aunt JoJo, whom Kayla had mentioned at the school open house?

Joelly Standish waggled her fingers at Holden's niece. "Hey, kiddo. Great to see you again."

"You, too," Holly said with a bit more enthusiasm. "Did you bring Sassy?"

The blonde shook her head. "We just dropped her at the groomer's." She swung a pink duffel from her shoulder and handed it to Kayla. Then she bent down and hugged the dark-haired girl. "Have fun, sweetie!"

"I will, Aunt JoJo," Kayla replied as she hugged her back and then wriggled free. "Thanks for having me over, Mr. Thomas," she said politely before running off with Holly. Their footsteps pounded on the stairs as they headed to Holly's room.

Holden turned toward the woman standing on his porch. "I thought I recognized you." He'd refrained from mentioning this in class, not wanting her to think he'd been trying to pick her up with a tired old line.

She shrugged. "Everybody recognizes me."

"Not from class. I thought I'd seen you before, like this." She wore jeans and a sweater now, instead of the short skirts and tight blouses she sported most of the time. Her hair was in a high ponytail and black-rimmed glasses were perched on her nose. "You were at the open house at school. You're Aunt JoJo—Roberta's best friend."

"BFF."

"What?"

She shrugged again. "Nothing. I thought you'd be at the shelter and that Mrs. Crayden would be here."

"And I thought you'd be Roberta." Even though he'd agreed they should not see each other anymore, he'd wanted to see her. He'd been looking forward to it.

"She's having car issues, so I offered to drop off Kayla." A pink SUV, undoubtedly hers, was parked at the curb in front of the house. "Why aren't you working?"

"Holly asked…more like begged me to stay home tonight and spend some time with her and Kayla." Since he already felt guilty for spending so much time at the shelter, he hadn't had the heart to refuse her.

Joelly Standish grinned, then chuckled.

"What?"

"You're being played," she said.

He furrowed his brow, confused. "I don't understand."

"I think you and Robbie have a couple of matchmakers on your hands," she warned him.

"No." But even as he denied it, he realized she was probably right. Holly had been singing Roberta's praises ever since she'd spent the night at the vice cop's home.

"Okay, whatever. Just remember that I warned you," Joelly said. "So are you going to be here in the morning when Robbie comes to pick her up?"

"No. I'll be at the shelter." He would make certain of it. "Mrs. Crayden will be here."

He'd been weak tonight because he'd wanted to see Robbie again—just to confirm the fact that he'd imagined his attraction to her, he told himself. But now he intended to stick to their agreement. He had to.

The mayor's daughter was probably right in thinking that his niece was playing matchmaker, but it was just because she wanted a mom. She didn't even know Roberta Meyers.

He wished *he* didn't know her, wished he had no idea what she tasted like, how sweet, how passionate…

He had been crazy to kiss her; his body still ached for her. But he'd hurt more, and so would Holly, if Roberta wound up on that memorial wall in the lobby of the police station. After witnessing more than once her dedication to her job, he feared it was damn likely that she would.

ROBBIE'S HEART POUNDED as she hammered her fist on the front door of the stone-and-brick Tudor. Her daughter's voice, quavering and fearful, echoed in her head. She had never heard Kayla sound so frightened before. The minute the door opened, she pushed her way inside. "What did you do to her?"

"What...?" Holden rubbed the sleep from his eyes.

Robbie's gaze skimmed over his tousled hair and down his bare chest to the pajama bottoms hanging low on his thin hips. And now her heart pounded even harder against her ribs. "Kayla—what did you do to my daughter? She called me, hysterical, and begged me to come get her."

Shock and concern brought him fully awake. "I thought they were sound asleep. I didn't even know she called you." He turned toward the ornate staircase in the center hall. "They're upstairs."

Anxiously she ran up the steps. Kayla rarely spent the night away from her—maybe across the hall at Joelly's or upstairs at Brenda the college student's—but never with a virtual stranger. Even though Holden only lived a few blocks away, her daughter had been too far from Robbie's loving arms.

Holden followed Robbie, his long strides closing the distance between them. On the second-story landing, he passed her and led the way down the hall, pushing open a bedroom door. "They're sleeping," he said again.

Brushing against his bare chest, Robbie shoved past him. Light from the hall illuminated the room and the two little girls who shared a full-size canopy bed. Holly's face was buried in her pillow and Kayla lay on her back, her rosebud lips parted as she breathed evenly. Too evenly, without the faintest hitch...

Legs trembling in reaction to her mad flight to Holden's house, Robbie crossed the room. She knelt at Kayla's side of the bed.

"Sweetheart?" she whispered, running her fingertips along her daughter's cheek. It was dry and warm with no trace of the tears she'd heard in the child's tremulous voice when she'd called.

"She's fine," Holden said from the doorway.

"Kayla?" Robbie prodded her, needing her daughter's assurance, not his.

"Mommy?" her daughter murmured as she shifted against the pillow.

"I came, sweetheart, to take you home." She struggled to control her emotions. Whenever Kayla cried, Robbie had to fight tears of her own. "Like you wanted."

Kayla shook her head. "Now I wanna stay."

"Sweetheart, you called and said you wanted me to take you home," Robbie reminded her. *She* wanted to take her daughter home, too, for without Kayla, the apartment felt so empty, and Robbie felt so alone.

"It was just a bad dream," Kayla assured her. "I'm okay now."

Robbie stroked her fingers over her daughter's silky hair. "What was your bad dream about?" Had Kayla noticed the bruises on her mother's throat? Was she scared that she'd nearly lost her?

Kayla's delicate shoulders moved in a shrug. "I don't remember. I'm so tired." She had yet to open her eyes. "I wanna go back to sleep. Let me stay, Mommy."

Robbie's heart clutched. Her daughter so rarely called her Mommy anymore, convinced she was too old to refer to her mother the way a *baby* would. Robbie leaned over and pressed a kiss to Kayla's forehead. "You're sure you don't want to come home with me?"

Kayla nodded, her hair rustling against the pillowcase. "I wanna stay with Holly and Uncle Holden."

"Mr. Thomas," Robbie automatically corrected her, alarmed that the child had grown so close to him in one evening. Apparently he had that effect on all females...

"I wanna stay," Kayla said again as she snuggled into the pillow.

"It'll be for the best," Holden said. "You don't want to wake her up and drag her out this late. Just let her stay."

She kissed Kayla's cheek now. "I love you, baby. Call me if you change your mind." And she'd come here every bit as quickly as she had the first time.

She eased up from the floor, her gaze never leaving her daughter's peaceful face. Had she imagined the hysteria in Kayla's voice when she'd called? There wasn't even a trace of tears on the child's face. Robbie edged back toward the door, where Holden was leaning against the jamb. She passed him, this time careful not to touch him, and left the bedroom.

He closed the door and turned toward her. "You did the right thing, letting her stay."

Robbie shook her head, not trusting herself to speak. Her arms ached with the need to hold her child, to offer the comfort that Kayla had seemed to need when she'd called.

Holden reached out and wrapped his fingers around her wrist, then tugged her down the hall—not toward the stairs but away from them. Before she could react, he'd pulled her through an open doorway into a dimly lit room. A lamp burned beside a rumpled, king-size bed.

She wrenched her wrist free of his grasp and whirled on him. "Why the hell did you bring me in here?"

It was obviously the master bedroom, probably bigger

than her entire apartment and definitely more elegant with its cherry-paneled walls. The draperies and bed-spread, in a deep chocolate, matched and added to the masculinity of the room. The man standing half-naked before her surpassed the masculinity of the room, with his bare chest and the low-slung flannel pajama bottoms.

He shoved the door shut with an open palm, then reached for her. "Not for this," he said, even as he pulled her against his taut body. Then he lowered his head and covered her mouth with his.

She wedged her hands between them, intending to push him away. But her palms skimmed over bare skin and hard muscle, and her own skin tingled. Her pulse raced with excitement. Beneath her touch, his heart pounded hard and fast.

Why was it that they lost control every time they came together? The reaction was more powerful than mere attraction or infatuation, but she refused to label it. For the moment she just wanted to enjoy. She'd missed him.

She opened her mouth and invited him in; his tongue slid over hers. He tasted of mint and man. She clenched her fingers, kneading the muscles of his chest. Soft hair brushed her skin.

Desire slammed through her so powerfully that a moan began to burn in her throat. He slid his hands down her back to the curve of her hips, pulling her tight against his straining erection. Her legs trembled. As if he sensed her weakening, he lifted her and carried her to the bed.

"This is crazy," she said as she sank onto a feather duvet and soft pillows.

"I know," he agreed, even as his gaze, eyes dark with passion, moved over her like a caress.

"We agreed to stay away from each other," she reminded him.

"I've missed seeing you," he said, his voice rough with desire. "I missed tasting you, touching you…" His fingers slid to the bottom edge of her sweater, toying with the slightly frayed hem. Her breath caught in her throat as he began to ease the fabric up over her stomach. He leaned over and kissed her navel, dipping his tongue into the indentation.

She touched him, too, smoothing her fingers over the sinewy muscles in his arms and shoulders. As busy as he was, she was surprised he found time to work out, but he probably had a gym in his house—it was big enough—or at the shelter.

Meeting her gaze, he watched her as he shifted her sweater higher over the satin cups of her bra. He traced his fingertips along the edges of the cups, where her breasts spilled over the top. Then he touched the front clasp, pushing against it until it popped loose. The undergarment fell open, baring her breasts.

He groaned. "You're beautiful, more beautiful than I imagined."

Her lips twitched into a smile. "You've thought about me naked?"

He groaned again. "More than I wanted."

Pressure built inside her, and her femininity throbbed with the same urgency as his erection. He cupped her, teasing her nipples with his palms. She arched, pressing against him and wanting more.

He tore his mouth from hers. Then his lips touched

her breasts, pressing kisses against the sensitive skin until he reached a nipple. His tongue stroked across one tip while his thumb teased the other.

"Please," she murmured, needing more—needing him to release the pressure spiraling inside her. "Please…"

But he lifted his head, his muscles tensing. "Did you hear that?"

"What?" She listened but could hear nothing other than her own blood rushing through her body.

His handsome face drawn taut, as if it nearly killed him, he eased away from her and rolled off the bed. Then he stalked over to the door and pressed his ear to the wood. He pushed his hand through his hair and shook his head. "I thought I heard something…"

"What was it—the sound of my common sense sailing out the window?" she asked.

His lips quirked into a wry grin. "Your common sense? I thought that was mine." He turned back to her, to how she lay on his rumpled bed, and his grin faded away. Then he expelled a ragged breath, leaning back against the door. "We had an agreement."

"To stay away from each other," she reminded them both as she reclasped her bra and pulled down her sweater. But it didn't matter that she'd covered up; she could still feel his mouth on her. She still ached inside, longing for more.

"I intended to stick to that agreement," he said earnestly.

"So if you didn't bring me in here for…" She patted the bed as she rose from it.

He shook his head. "I didn't."

She found her shoes, realizing only now that they'd fallen off, and stepped into them. "Then why *did* you bring me in here?"

That grin flashed across his face again. "I wanted to talk to you, and I didn't want to wake the kids."

She pulled her bottom lip between her teeth. It tasted of him. "I should have taken her home."

"Your daughter is fine," he said, reaching for her once more.

But Robbie pulled back. If he touched her, they'd wind up back in his bed, and she doubted that they would regain their senses. She couldn't be selfish and focus on her needs; she had to think about Kayla. "I'm not sure that she's fine. She never has nightmares. I don't think she feels safe here."

"She's safe here," he said tersely. "I don't think it's my house that made her feel insecure."

"What are you saying?"

He bit his lip, too, as if holding back what he really wanted to say. She didn't need to hear the words to know what he thought.

"You'll never accept my job," she said.

"No," he replied. "I can't."

Although she flinched inwardly, she managed to shrug as if she didn't care. "It's really not that dangerous…"

He shook his head. "Just since I've met you, you've been shot at and almost strangled."

"Those were wild shots—".

"That I hear fired often down by the shelter. The streets are dangerous for runaways and the cops who police them." He pushed a hand through his hair. "As proved by those videos they showed in class."

Send For
2 FREE BOOKS
Today!

I accept your offer!

Please send me two free *Harlequin American Romance®* novels and two mystery gifts (gifts worth about $10). I understand that these books are completely free— even the shipping and handling will be paid—and I am under no obligation to purchase anything, ever, as explained on the back of this card.

354 HDL EYU2   154 HDL EYPR

Please Print

FIRST NAME

LAST NAME

ADDRESS

APT.#   CITY

STATE/PROV.   ZIP/POSTAL CODE

Visit us online at
www.ReaderService.com

Offer limited to one per household and not valid to current subscribers of *Harlequin American Romance®* books.

Your Privacy — Harlequin Books is committed to protecting your privacy. Our Privacy Policy is available online at www.eHarlequin.com or upon request from the Harlequin Reader Service. From time to time we make our list of customers available to reputable third parties who may have a product or service of interest to you. If you would prefer for us not to share your name and address, please check here ☐.

▶ Detach card and mail today. No stamp needed. ▶

H-AR-09/09

"Being a cop isn't a death sentence," she insisted.

"That's not what the memorial in the police station lobby implies."

"Given how long the Lakewood Police Department's existed, there haven't been many officers who've died," she pointed out. "Although even one is too many."

"Someday your picture could be a part of that memorial." He shuddered.

"I'm careful."

He shook his head, his jaw clenched. "No, you're not. You've been lucky."

Anger burned now, heating her blood just as desire for him had moments ago. "I'm good at my job."

"I was the one who had the nightmare tonight," he said, "remembering you in that alley, getting the life choked out of you."

"And I defended myself," she reminded him.

"Even if nothing ever happened to you I'd be the one worrying every time you left for work, thinking that you might get hurt. Or that you might not come back at all. I lived through years of that worry over my sister. I can't go through it again."

"I heard you the first time you told me that," she said.

He gestured toward the rumpled bed. "I had to remind myself."

She summoned her pride and headed toward the door. As she pulled it open, she turned back and promised him, "I won't let you forget again."

He didn't say anything as he followed her downstairs and opened the door for her.

"I'll ask Joelly to pick Kayla up tomorrow morning," she said. "We'll stick to our agreement from now on."

His eyes dark with regret, he nodded.

But as Robbie walked out to the borrowed SUV, she worried that it was too late. She'd already begun to fall for a man who had vowed he would never love her.

Chapter Nine

As Holden surveyed the dining hall, tension pounded in his temples and the base of his head. In the six months since he'd opened the shelter, he'd never seen so many empty tables. The new metal detectors, no matter how discreet, had scared away some of the regulars. Or else the increase in number and decrease in age of the security guards had. Students at Lakewood University's Police Academy, the guards were nearly the same age as the kids they were assigned to protect. The chief of police had recommended them.

Of course Holden wouldn't have considered any of the changes if not for Robbie. And most of the kids at the shelter knew it. They grumbled their complaints around bites of food as he joined some kids from his morning youth group.

"It's startin' to feel like juvie around here," Todd griped, "with all the cops."

"They're not cops." Not yet. He really wanted to ask the kid how he knew what juvie was like, but the teens were already skittish. He didn't want to scare off more of them with an interrogation.

"But you're doing all this because of that chick cop," Todd said as he lifted a sandwich to his mouth.

"That lady cop is a real bitch," Skylar added. The fifteen-year-old's green eyes hardened with bitterness. Holden was glad she hadn't left the shelter like so many others had. The streets were infinitely more dangerous for her, a pretty, young girl. She reminded him so much of Lorielle.

"Officer Meyers was just doing her job," Holden said.

Around another bite of his turkey sandwich, Todd mumbled, "Her job sucks."

"Her job is to make the streets safer for you, and she takes that responsibility very seriously." Remembering her grappling with that drug dealer in the alley, he flinched. "It's a tough job. And you have to be a tough person to want to do it."

Todd laughed. "Hey, the rev's got a crush on the hot chick cop."

Skylar's eyes rounded with horror. "No, no, he can't. He doesn't…"

Holden hoped it *was* only a crush. Then it would be easy to get over. *She'd* be easy to get over. He shook his head. "Not at all."

"What about *that* chick, Rev?" Todd asked with a soft whistle. He gestured toward one of the volunteers, a familiar-looking blonde. Joelly Standish.

As if she'd felt their attention, she lifted her head and waved.

Color flooded Todd's thin face. "You know her?"

Holden nodded. "Yes. And I'm going to go say hello. Excuse me."

"Oh, the rev's a player," Todd teased, and then yelped when Skylar punched his arm. Holden left them squabbling as he walked off to join Joelly.

He had the sudden urge to revert to high-school tactics and ask her best friend what Robbie had said about him. If the two women were as close as Kayla had claimed, did they share everything? Had Robbie told her about their kisses? About the fire that burned between them anytime they were together?

Instead, he said, "I thought it was just the school open house that I recognized you from, but you've been here before, haven't you? You volunteer."

"Not as much as I should," Joelly admitted ruefully. "It's been a while."

"Because you stay busy helping Roberta with Kayla?"

"Robbie takes care of her daughter by herself, but I do help her when I can," Joelly said. "I work nights, so I sleep most of the day away." She pushed a hand through her tousled hair. "Obviously I didn't sleep much today."

"A gentleman would assure you that you look well rested," he said, but he had noted the dark circles beneath her eyes.

She chuckled. "You're a minister—you're not supposed to lie."

"Actually I didn't finish at the seminary. I'm only a counselor," he corrected her. "The pastor of St. Mike's called me the youth minister, and then the kids started calling me *Reverend* there. It just stuck."

"You earned the title. You really care about these kids," she said, pressing a fist against her mouth as she yawned. "Sorry…"

"You work nights."

"Shh, don't tell anyone," she said with a mischievous smile. "I'd hate to ruin the public's image of me being an all-night party girl."

"Why?" He gestured at her casual clothes. "I don't understand why you dress differently for the Citizens' Police Academy."

"I started dressing like that when I was about the age of most of these kids," she said, "to irritate my father. Then I kind of got myself trapped in that image because it's what people expected of the princess of Lakewood."

"People can change," he encouraged her.

Sadness flashed in her eyes. "Sometimes other people won't let them."

"You're old enough not to care what other people think," he pointed out.

"You obviously haven't met my father."

"As a matter of fact, I have." And he would again at the mayor's ball.

"Then you know there's no age limit on caring what other people think of you."

"Does anyone at the Lakewood PD know that you and Roberta are friends?" he asked. He couldn't recall them interacting in class.

"Please don't tell anyone," she implored. "I don't want my reputation to affect how her fellow officers regard Robbie."

"You're not exactly their favorite person," he said, gently. "But it's not personal. It's just because of the position your dad has taken about hiring more police."

"Yeah, I know, but sometimes it feels personal," she admitted. He saw a flash of hurt on her face.

"I have a personal question," he said.

She sighed, but acquiesced. "Ask away."

"You said you didn't spend as much time here as you should," he recalled. "Why *should* you spend time here?"

"I just… I know where these kids are coming from," she said.

"You were a runaway like Robbie?"

Surprise widened her eyes. "She told you?"

"Yes."

"She doesn't like to talk about it." Joelly sighed again. "Neither do I. There wasn't a place like this…back then." She smiled with satisfaction as she glanced around the shelter. "You've done a good thing here, Reverend Thomas."

The high-pitched beeping of the metal detectors drew their attention to the man who'd just walked through the door. He wore a Lakewood PD uniform and a German shepherd walked at his side. Despite their wariness of police officers, the kids swarmed him. No doubt because of the dog.

Joelly stammered, "I—I have to go now."

Holden barely managed to say goodbye before she grabbed her tray and headed into the kitchen. Was it just coincidence that it was in the opposite direction from Sergeant Ethan Brewer?

"She sure didn't stick around long," Sergeant Brewer commented with a nod toward the swinging doors, as Holden joined him and his K9 partner.

"Who?"

"Joelly Standish," he said. "That was her, right, in that disguise?"

"Disguise?" Holden echoed.

"The baggy jeans and sweater."

"You know, I think that might be how she really dresses," Holden said. The short skirts and tight shirts were the true disguise. He could commiserate with Joelly on the subject of complicated family dynamics. While his mother had resented his relationship with his half sister, his father had resented his decision to become a youth minister, rather than following him into the family business. But he'd had no interest in running marina franchises along the Lake Michigan coast.

The sergeant shook his head. "I don't know what to believe about the princess, except that my sisters are probably right. I need a low-maintenance woman." He sighed. "And I don't think they get much higher-maintenance than Joelly Standish. It'd be crazy to even think about her...like that."

"Crazy," Holden agreed, but he was really thinking about himself and Roberta Meyers. And he had to *stop* thinking about her, about kissing her, touching her—

"Yeah," Ethan said, albeit with a trace of disappointment. "It's better to stick with someone you have something in common with. Bullet—uh, Sergeant Terlecki—mentioned that you're dating Meredith Wallingford?" He whistled in appreciation, and the sound immediately caused his dog, who was being petted, to lift his head and perk up his ears. Some silent communication passed between the partners, then the German shepherd relaxed and went back to soaking up the kids' attention. "She's gorgeous."

Maybe it was because Holden had known Meredith for so long that he hadn't realized how attractive she'd become. "Yes, she is," he concurred with a sense of bemusement.

Ethan nodded. "She's perfect for you, too. She can help you out with the shelter. She really understands what you're trying to do." He glanced toward the kitchen door through which Joelly had disappeared a short time before. "People don't get that writing checks isn't enough."

Holden could have corrected the sergeant's misconception about Joelly, but he didn't want to betray her confidence. Instead, he said, "I'm sure you'll meet someone special," even as he suspected the officer already had.

Brewer sighed. "It's not always easy finding someone who can handle being with a cop."

"Really?" So he wasn't the only one who'd found it a problem.

"Yeah, it's long hours and not the greatest pay."

"What about the danger?"

Ethan laughed. "There are some who find that exciting, like that college girl in the CPA." He sighed. "Then there are others who wouldn't even consider dating a cop because of it."

Like Holden.

"Whoa," Ethan said with a laugh. "Sorry for getting all Dear Abby on you. I just came by to check out the shelter. The chief mentioned you were making some changes. The metal detector and the interns are great ideas."

"They weren't mine." Holden sighed. "But they were necessary. Too bad the metal detectors can't detect narcotics. If only there was some way to check for drugs without frisking every kid as he comes through the doors. I've already been told this place is getting to be like juvie. And that was never my intention."

"Yeah, I know you had the best intentions." Ethan pointed toward his dog. "Jaws and I can help you out from time to time. He'll pick up on anyone carrying something they shouldn't have."

"Thank you," Holden said, "for everything." Not only had the sergeant helped him find a solution to the problem that bothered him most, but he'd also given him perspective on Meredith.

After Ethan and Jaws left, Holden slipped into his office to make a call. "Meredith," he said the moment she picked up, "I'm sure. You're the one I want to take to the mayor's ball."

If only she was the woman he *wanted*.

"PLEASE, MOM, can't Holly come over tonight? Brenda can watch us both. Her uncle is never around, and she gets lonely in that big, old house all alone." Kayla stood in the doorway to the bathroom, watching Robbie apply mascara to her lashes.

Usually she didn't bother with much makeup, unless she was working undercover, but tonight was the mayor's ball. In addition to the makeup, she wore one of Joelly's old gowns. Fortunately they were the same size, so the silvery blue silk fit well.

"Holly isn't all alone," Robbie said, careful to keep her sympathy for Holden's orphaned niece from her face. She was pretty certain Kayla was manipulating her, just as she had last weekend with her "nightmare."

When Robbie had had time to think clearly, she'd realized that Kayla's face couldn't have been that dry, her voice that clear, unless she'd been faking her hysterical phone call.

"She has Mrs. Crayden, and she seems very nice, very grandmotherly."

Her daughter's brow furrowed in confusion. "What do you mean?"

Of course Kayla had no experience with grandmothers, Joelly's socialite mother being the closest thing to one that Kayla had ever known. Mrs. Standish, despite the years Robbie had lived with her, had always kept her distance emotionally and physically, not just from Robbie but from Joelly, too.

"I'm sure she gives Holly a lot of attention and affection," Robbie explained.

Kayla shook her head. "No. She's really just their housekeeper. And besides, she's old."

"Kayla!" Robbie admonished her daughter. "She's not old." She was probably only in her early fifties, at the most.

Her daughter eyed her dubiously. "Well, she's not fun like you are."

"Sucking up will get you nowhere," Robbie insisted. "And anyway, I will be out with Aunt JoJo, so Holly won't be able to have fun with me." While she didn't want to damage her daughter's friendship with Holly, Robbie didn't want to get any more attached to the child herself. Holden didn't think she'd be good for his niece. Or himself.

"You look like a princess, Mommy." Kayla continued to pour on the charm. "I wish…"

"It's a grown-up party," Robbie explained, "otherwise I'd take you."

"Since I can't go, let me have Holly come over. Her uncle can drop her off."

And see Robbie all dressed up? Was that her daughter's plan? Robbie shook her head, disappointed in herself. She had grown far too cynical if she suspected her own daughter's motives. "I've paid Brenda to babysit just you."

"We'll play together, so it'll be easier for her than watching just me." Kayla's rosebud lips pulled into a pout. "I really wanna hang out with Holly."

"You hang out with Holly at school every day," Robbie reminded her. "You'll have to wait until next weekend." She shook her head. "No, I'm working next weekend. The weekend after that."

Kayla complained, "You're always working."

"I just had a few days off, remember?"

"Probably just because you got hurt." The nine-year-old grimaced, and pain dimmed the brightness of her blue eyes. "Again."

Robbie's breath caught. Was Holden right? Did her job cause her daughter anxiety? "Don't you like my job?"

Kayla shrugged. "I don't like you working nights. I only see you for a couple of hours when I get out of school. And it really sucks when you work weekends."

"So it's my shift you don't like?"

The girl shrugged again.

"You're okay with my job, though? It doesn't bother you?" Or give her nightmares as Holden had implied?

"No." Kayla smiled. Even though disappointed that she hadn't gotten her way, she wasn't a sulker. "Kids think I'm really cool when I say my mom's a cop."

Robbie pulled her daughter close for a hug. "I think you're cool, too, but because you're you. Not because of what your mom does for a living."

"Holly likes me for me, too," Kayla added. "She's my best friend."

"Just your friend," she said, "not your sister like you two have been telling the rest of the class." The teacher's phone call had enlightened Robbie about the two friends' matchmaking scheme.

Kayla's face flushed. "Mrs. Groom called?"

Robbie nodded, her eyes narrowed as she met her daughter's gaze. "What's that all about?"

"It's just a joke," Kayla insisted. "Mrs. Groom has no sense of humor."

"Okay, just so you know…"

"Of course I know we're not sisters."

"And you're not going to be sisters." Robbie wasn't good enough to be Holden's wife or Holly's mother.

WITH SASSY CURLED UP on her lap, Kayla sat cross-legged on the zebra rug on Aunt JoJo's wood floor. Her fingers trembling with nerves, she stroked the dog's fur as she carried out her and Holly's Plan B. "Mom's busy getting ready, too, so she asked if you could call Mr. Thomas for her, about dropping Holly off to spend the night tonight."

Her heart pounded as she watched Aunt JoJo slide her feet into super-high heels. Her aunt hated wearing shoes. She and Mom would be leaving soon. And then Uncle Holden wouldn't have a chance to see Mom dressed up like a movie star.

"She did?" Joelly asked, and she did that thing where just one eyebrow formed an arch.

Kayla had tried it before in the mirror, but she couldn't raise just one; both went up and wrinkled her forehead. "Yeah. She's gotta finish her makeup, so she wondered if you could do it for her."

"I know what you're up to, kiddo," Aunt JoJo said, and now her caramel-colored eyes went all squinty as she stared at Kayla.

She shifted her butt on the rug, which wrinkled on the hardwood floor. Sassy jumped off her lap. Mom had that look, too—the one Aunt Jo was giving her—and it always made her squirm until she confessed all. But this was too important for her to chicken out now. She was going to prove to those kids at school that she and Holly weren't lying. They really were sisters—or would be soon.

She fluttered her lashes and pretended she had no idea what her aunt was talking about. "I'm not up to anything."

"Yes, you are, sweetie," Aunt JoJo said with a knowing smile. "You're trying to set up your mom with your friend's uncle."

"N-n-no…" Kayla stammered, her nerves running wild. Every time she lied she got caught; no wonder she didn't try it much.

"Actually I don't think it's a bad idea at all." Joelly sighed and shook her head. "But your mom does."

"Holly's uncle is really nice, though." Mr. Thomas would be a great dad. He'd been so nice when she spent the night, telling her to make herself at home and making sure she had everything she needed. But she hadn't had the guts to tell him what she really needed, what she had needed for nine years—a *dad*.

"Yes, he is nice. But that doesn't mean he and your mom would get along."

"They do argue sometimes," Kayla admitted, "except when they're kissing."

"Kissing?" Aunt Jo asked, her eyes wide with shock and then delight. "Kissing? Really?"

Kayla nodded again. "I saw it myself in our apartment. And when I spent the night at Holly's, we got Mom to come over—"

"But *I* dropped you off—" Joelly's forehead frowned "—and picked you up from Holly's."

Kayla's face got hot as she confessed, "I called her in the middle of the night pretending I had a nightmare."

Aunt JoJo laughed. "They kissed that night, too?"

"I don't know, but they went into his bedroom for a while. We were gonna listen at the door, but the floor's so squeaky we were afraid we'd get caught."

"Oh, someone's been holding out on me." Joelly laughed again. "Call your friend. You'll find out that her uncle is also going to the ball tonight." Her eyes twinkled. "I made sure he got an invitation."

Kayla's mouth fell open in shock. "You're trying to get them together, too."

"Yes." Then she mumbled, so low that Kayla could barely catch her words, "At least one of us deserves to get the good guy."

Again Kayla's mouth fell open in shock, and then dread. "Do you like Mr. Thomas, too?" She didn't want him for an uncle; she wanted him for a dad.

Joelly shook her head. "No, but I think he's nice."

"I wish Mom thought so."

"She thinks something of him, since she's been kissing him," Joelly said.

Kayla's heart warmed with hope. "Yes, she does…" Maybe she loved him.

Chapter Ten

"I'm surprised to see you here," a feminine voice said. When Holden turned to the woman the first thing he noticed was the turmoil in her eyes, the love and regret.

"Hi, Mom." He leaned over and kissed her cheek. Her perfectly manicured fingers grasped the sleeves of his tux.

"It's wonderful you're here," she said, blinking back a hint of moisture. "And with Meredith." She released him to embrace Merry.

She looked beautiful tonight, gorgeous, in fact, as Ethan Brewer had said. Her reddish-orange gown complemented her willowy body and sleek brown hair. Holden should have been proud she'd agreed to be his date. But he thought of Holly, instead, his heart heavy with regret. His niece had been so disappointed that he was taking someone other than Kayla's mom to the ball. Since she was always such an optimistic child, her tears had struck him especially hard. She hadn't cried like that since her mother died. If only she could understand that he was doing this for her...

His father, his arm around his wife's waist, extended

a hand to Holden. "Everyone's been talking about you, son, praising the work you're doing at the shelter."

Shock staggered Holden. His father had called him an idealistic fool for throwing away his life for a hopeless cause. Years earlier the man had referred to his daughter the same way—hopeless. Remembering this had anger and resentment pressing on Holden's lungs. He had to fight for breath. "Excuse me," he said. "I—I need some air."

Moisture filled his mother's eyes again. "It's crowded in here," she said, despite the fact that the mayor's mansion could have held more than the two hundred or so guests who attended the ball. "You get some air. We'll wait here for you."

He nodded and crossed the room, with its gleaming marble floors, to step through one of the open, sliding glass doors overlooking the lake. He walked out onto the deck and breathed deeply.

Maybe he *had* just needed air and hadn't needed to escape his father's hypocrisy. But he doubted it.

The deck was as crowded as the house; people were lined up at the bar on one end. He walked toward the other end, where only a few people stood near the railing, watching the water reflect the orange glow of the setting sun.

He released a soft sigh at the beauty of the view. And not just of the water. A woman wearing a silvery blue dress that molded itself to the full curves of her petite body stood at the railing. Her hair, a riot of dark curls, spilled down her back. Tonight Roberta Meyers was yet another woman, a stunning beauty.

A bald, older man in a white tuxedo broke away

from a group of people and approached her. She turned from the railing and threw her arms around his neck. And Holden gasped, as if someone had slugged him hard in the stomach.

ROBBIE INHALED the sweet scent of Joel Standish's spicy cologne before loosening her arms from around his neck and stepping back. "Do you greet all your party crashers with a hug?" she teased.

He chuckled. "This is your home, honey. You can't crash a party at your own home."

She smiled, wishing she could accept that this was really her home, but she had never felt as if she belonged here. Regrettably the mayor's daughter had always felt the same way. "So you don't mind my showing up uninvited?"

"You know you never need an invitation. You don't come around nearly enough as it is," he admonished her, tapping his fingertip on the tip of her nose. "I'm delighted you're here."

"You might regret that," she warned.

He groaned. "Oh, Joelly's already been giving me the business about the police department. *Et tu?*" He laughed. "Of course, you two have always been like peas in a pod." The grin slid from his face. "She told me you got hurt because I won't approve Archer's hiring more officers." He touched the silk scarf that matched her borrowed dress. "Is that the truth?"

Maybe he knew his daughter better than Robbie realized. "It's the truth that the Lakewood PD is understaffed and that puts every officer in the department in danger." She touched the scarf, too. "But this was my own fault. I chased down a suspect on my own without calling for backup first."

"Roberta Meyers!" he exclaimed, causing several guests to turn toward them and stare. His bellow, despite his smaller stature, was no less formidable than the chief's. "What the hell were you thinking?"

Her lips twitched into a smile.

"You think that's funny? To put your life at risk like that?"

"No." She thought it was funny how similar Joel Standish was to his archenemy, Frank Archer. "Of course not." Even though it would kill her to let a suspect get away, she would definitely be more careful in the future.

"So what happened?"

"I was visiting the shelter and recognized someone…" Feeling a familiar gaze on her, she glanced up and scanned the guests gathered on the deck. Many of them stared back, but then everyone watched the mayor. He had that kind of magnetic personality, the kind that had kept getting him elected term after term after term. Only one person was watching her. Her pulse tripped, then raced at the sight of him in a black tuxedo with a pleated white shirt setting off his tan and the breeze ruffling his hair. "Holden…"

The mayor followed her gaze to the youth minister. "Joelly had me add him to the guest list."

"Of course she did," Robbie said. "Your daughter is more like you than you think."

He chuckled and put an arm around her shoulders as Holden approached them. He stuck out his free hand. "Reverend Thomas, I'm glad you could make it tonight."

"It was an honor to be invited, sir," Holden smoothly responded. "I cannot tell you how much I appreciate your donations to the shelter. You've really helped a lot of runaways."

"Yes, he has," Robbie agreed.

The mayor squeezed her shoulders. "Not as many as the reverend has. Your shelter is quite impressive."

"It's getting there." Holden's gaze slid to Robbie. "It was recently brought to my attention that it needed some improvements."

The mayor glanced down at her, then over at Holden and back. "I take it this girl here made the suggestions. Be careful, Reverend, she and my daughter are forces of nature."

"Thank you for the warning, sir," Holden said, smiling. "And again for the donations."

"I'll leave you two young people to visit," the mayor said. "I have to make the rounds of my constituents. Shake hands, kiss…cheeks."

Holden chuckled. But Robbie found no amusement in having her former guardian leave them alone. Although she clutched at Joel's tuxedo jacket, he pulled away and walked off.

"I wondered if you'd be here," Holden said, "since you and Joelly are friends. But I didn't realize how well you knew the mayor."

"I used to live here," she admitted, turning back to lean over the railing and stare out at the sparkling surface of the lake.

"It's quite a view," he said as he propped his elbows on the railing next to her. He stared at her, though, instead of the water.

"Yes, it's nice, but I'm leaving now," she said. "Just want to walk on the beach first." She'd done her part to influence the mayor. Hell, she'd done more than Joelly had. She wasn't even sure her friend had shown up, since at the last minute, they'd decided to drive separately. She headed toward the stairs leading down to the beach. One quick walk in the sand, and she'd drive herself home.

Heavy footsteps sounded behind her. "It's cold," Holden said, "and your shoes…"

She stopped on the last stair before the sand and reached down for her borrowed heels. How the hell did Joelly wear these things so often? She hooked the straps around her finger and stepped onto the beach. Cool sand filtered between her toes. "You don't have to join me," she said. "I'd actually prefer if you didn't. It kind of flies in the face of that whole staying-away-from-each-other pact we got going."

"I'm afraid that's not the only thing we've got going," Holden said. He caught her hand and linked their fingers. "I want to stay away from you. I really want—" he stopped moving and tugged Robbie to an abrupt halt "—you."

"No, you don't. You couldn't handle dating me," she reminded him. "All that uncertainty, the danger." Yet she was in more danger here on a moonlit beach with Holden than she'd ever been on the job. She was in danger of falling in love.

"You're so beautiful." He stared down at her, his eyes wide with wonder. "So damn beautiful." He lowered his head until his lips brushed hers.

Although the kiss was brief, Robbie shivered in

reaction. Holden stepped back and shrugged out of his jacket. Then he draped it around her shoulders. His warmth and masculine scent enveloped her.

"You *are* cold," he said.

She shook her head. "No. I'm confused. You keep pushing me away, then pulling me back."

"I know, I know. I'm confused, too. I know you're not right for me, for Holly, but—" he leaned down and kissed her again "—I want you."

Desire for him warmed her more than his jacket. "Holden…" Maybe it was the moonlight or how handsome he looked in a tux or just him, but she let down that wall the chief had talked about. She dropped her shoes on the sand and looped her arms around his neck and rose on tiptoe to kiss him back. Parting her lips, she took the kiss deeper.

His fingers tangled in her hair as his tongue slid in and out from between her lips. He stepped closer, so that not an inch separated their bodies.

She clutched his back and arched against him, pushing her breasts and hips against his tautly muscled body.

He groaned and pulled away, panting for breath. "Robbie…"

The desire in his rough voice echoed the desire building inside her. "What are we doing?" she asked, tipping her head back to stare up at the sky as if there were answers there. And she glimpsed someone standing at the deck railing, watching them. "Oh, God."

Holden followed her gaze to the deck. Not only was Meredith standing at the railing but his parents were, too, all staring down at them.

Robbie's hands shoved against his chest, which still labored for breath, and she broke away. "What the hell am I doing?" she whispered before turning and heading down the beach, away from the house.

He looked after her, tempted to follow. But footsteps on the stairs drew his attention back to the deck. Meredith descended to the beach. He crossed the sand to meet her. "I'm sorry," he murmured with guilt and regret.

Meredith laughed. "I knew there was something going on between you and Robbie."

"I wasn't hiding anything—"

"You were fighting it," she said. "And it looks like you're losing the battle."

He shook his head in denial. "I can't…I can't be with Robbie. We're not right for each other."

Meredith leaned close and pressed her lips to his cheek. "Neither are we, my friend." She stepped back and walked past him, heading off down the beach.

"Where are you going?"

"I'm going to talk to Robbie."

"Merry—"

She pointed up at the deck. "Tell your parents goodnight for me. They're ready to leave, but they wanted to talk to you first." Her smile flashed in the moonlight. "Good luck."

His legs heavy with reluctance, he climbed the stairs to the deck, where only his father waited for him. "Where's Mom?"

"She's using the powder room. She's not feeling well. That's why we decided to leave early," his father explained, tugging at the knot of his bow tie as if he'd suddenly gotten uncomfortable.

"Well, I should go find her," Holden said, "and tell her goodbye."

But Harold Thomas's hand grasped his arm, stopping him from rushing off. "We need to talk first."

He'd dropped the "son." Because of what he, and who knew how many other guests, had witnessed on the beach? "You shouldn't keep Mom waiting," Holden reminded him, "since she's not feeling well."

"This'll only take a moment, if you'll listen to me this time."

Holden clenched his jaw, knowing he was about to be subjected to another lecture. "Dad, this isn't the place—"

His father's grasp on his arm tightened. "Meredith's a good girl, from a good family."

"I know."

"She didn't deserve to be embarrassed like that," Harold Thomas reprimanded him. "What the hell were you thinking?"

"I wasn't," he admitted.

His father uttered a heavy sigh. "I've done that myself, son. Acted without thinking, and people wound up getting hurt."

"I know." In the beginning he'd been one of them. In the end Lorielle had been hurt the worst.

"So don't make the mistake I made."

"You don't even know her—"

"Roberta Meyers," his father said.

His mouth dropped open in surprise. "How do you know a vice cop?"

"Is that what she is now?" Harold asked with a faint hint of disdain.

"Yes. What do you know about her?"

"It was kept pretty quiet, so only a few people know. She's the dirty stray Standish's daughter dragged home from the streets, the pregnant runaway." His father's grasp tightened on his arm. "Stick with Meredith, son."

A gasp drew his attention to the stairs behind him, where Robbie stood, Meredith right behind her. She shoved his jacket into his hands and hurried off.

He started forward in pursuit, but his father, still gripping his arm, held him back. "Let her go," Harold advised. "She's a mistake you don't want to make."

"Let me go," Holden said. He didn't want the hypocrite touching him any longer. Maybe it was good he'd never finished at the seminary, because there were some lessons he was unable to preach—like forgive and forget.

Finally his father released him. "I'm going to go find your mother. She'd like to see you more. You need to come by the house more often."

Holden shook his head. "No, she wouldn't, because I won't come alone."

His father glanced behind him at Meredith, then glared at him. "You're not considering bringing that girl…"

"Your granddaughter? Yeah, I would bring her."

"Your mother…"

"Needs to accept that Holly is family. Your granddaughter. My niece. Actually my daughter now, since the adoption became official," Holden informed him. "If Mother wants me to come to brunch or dinner, she needs to invite Holly, too."

His father shook his head, his mouth twisted into a grimace of disappointment. "You always were so damn stubborn."

Holden bit his tongue, holding back his anger until

after his father walked off. Then he turned back to the railing and cursed.

"Shh," Meredith cautioned him. "You don't want the shelter's potential donors hearing you cuss."

He bent over and buried his face in his hands. His frustration wasn't only with his father. His body ached for Robbie's. "Why are you still here?" he asked.

"You're my ride, remember?" She smiled.

He turned his head to her. "You really are great."

"Yes, that's what everyone says."

So why couldn't he feel this attraction, this passion for her? He was a fool. "I don't deserve even your friendship."

"Funny, that's exactly what Robbie said. You two are so much alike." She nudged his shoulder with hers. "Don't listen to your father. Follow your heart. It's led you to the right places—to your sister, to Holly, to the shelter…"

He shook his head. It wasn't his heart that was leading him to Robbie, but he wouldn't make that crude admission to Meredith even though they were only friends. "I can't—"

"Don't make a liar out of me," Merry warned him.

"What?"

"I told her you're a great guy."

He would have liked to ask her to repeat their conversation word for word, but he'd already put his friend in a horrible position. "I don't deserve that, either."

She laughed. "It's uncanny really…"

"She said that, too?" Robbie must have been furious with him, especially if she'd overheard any of his father's lecture. And the sick churning in his stomach convinced him that she had.

"Here." She passed him the strap of the sandals Robbie had left on the beach. "Change her mind. Play Prince Charming to her Cinderella."

"Roberta Meyers is no Cinderella." Nor was she a dirty stray. "And I'm no Prince Charming."

Chapter Eleven

From the officers' table Robbie stared over the heads of the citizens and watched the door of the conference room. "Where is he?"

"The reverend's here already," Paddy O'Donnell said as he settled onto the chair next to her.

"Not him." She'd known the minute he'd entered the room—her skin tingled and her blood heated from just the touch of his glance. Ever since then, however, he'd avoided eye contact. "Billy. He's supposed to give the presentation about the vice unit. I'm just here—"

"—because I figured he'd try to bail on me, since I let his mom into the CPA," Paddy said.

So Holden hadn't complained about her in the statement he'd given to the watch commander. Maybe he wasn't a jerk, after all, if she believed what Meredith had told her on the beach, that she and Holden had only ever been friends.

"I didn't know why you wanted me to participate," she told the lieutenant. "I thought I might've done something wrong."

"Actually, you've done everything right," Paddy said. "You're a good cop."

"Thanks," she murmured with surprise. Asking her to participate had been more reward than punishment, she now realized, which made sense since the officers the watch commander usually recruited as CPA instructors had more experience on the job and in teaching than she did.

"Your phone's ringing," Paddy said.

She pulled the cell from her belt. It was just one of many accessories at her waist, like the nightstick, flashlight, pepper spray, Taser, gun, extra clip of ammo and cuffs. She didn't recognize the number on the caller ID screen. Had something happened to Kayla? "Hello?"

"Hey, Rob—"

"Billy?"

"Yeah, I need you to cover tonight's class."

Glancing at Marla Halliday, who sat in the second row near Holden, Robbie lowered her voice and asked, "Is it because your mom's in the class? Paddy thought you might skip out because of that."

A chuckle emanated from the phone. "No, that's not it. I can't leave without blowing my cover."

While Robbie had accepted her assignment to vice, she had insisted she couldn't go so deep undercover that she couldn't come home to Kayla.

"You're better at doing the instruction thing anyway," Billy said. "Probably because you're a mom."

"But I have no idea what to say." How, with Holden staring at her, could she talk about what had caused him so much pain? Even after what had happened the past weekend at the mayor's ball, she didn't want to bring up all those bad memories.

"You'll do great," Billy assured her as he hung up.

"Billy!" Only the dial tone was there.

"He couldn't make it?" Paddy asked.

She closed the phone and shook her head.

"So are you ready?" the watch commander asked.

"Ready?" She cleared her throat of the nerves tickling it. "I don't have anything prepared."

"It's nothing you can't handle," he said with a grin. "Remember, I wouldn't have asked you to be part of the program if you weren't a damn fine officer."

Touched by his praise, she summoned her pride and her guts and stood and approached the podium. She was a damn fine officer; she could handle anything to do with her job.

She stared out at the class, and her heart skipped a beat as she met Holden's gaze. *He* was what she couldn't handle: Holden and her feelings for him. No matter if he and Meredith were only friends, Robbie had to get over her feelings for the man. Because he would never accept her as she was, as a cop.

Holden leaned back in his chair so that he nearly touched the table behind him, the one at which Joelly Standish sat. He cocked his head and whispered, "Is everything all right with Kayla?"

Joelly snapped her cell phone shut and dropped it into her bag. Then she leaned forward and whispered back, as if they were in high school and she hoped the teacher wouldn't catch them talking, "Yeah. I just called the sitter. She's fine. That call was from someone else."

Even though he knew she could have been talking to

anyone, Holden couldn't stop himself from imagining it had been a man. And maybe she'd been making plans for later….

Lieutenant O'Donnell stepped to the podium, drawing Holden's and everyone else's attention. "Hey, folks, welcome to tonight's session about the vice unit. Once again Officer Roberta Meyers is pinch-hitting for the very busy sergeant of the vice division, Billy Halliday." He urged her forward with a hand on her back.

A muscle worked in Holden's jaw as he thought about the last time he'd touched her. How they'd slipped out of the ball to the beach below the mayor's mansion, and how he'd kissed her as though he would die if he didn't have a taste of her lips. And then he remembered the time before that, in his bed, as she lay almost naked in his arms. If only he hadn't heard a noise in the hall…

He had been a damn fool to stop. His body, still tense and aching, had yet to forgive him.

"Please bear with me," she beseeched with a smile as she adjusted the mike to her height. "I don't have anything formal prepared, but I'll try to tell you everything I know about the vice unit."

She knew a lot, Holden realized, as he listened to her talk about her job. Not only did she know what she was doing, but she obviously loved what she did. *Setting up buys, turning informants…getting drugs off the streets.*

If only she'd been able to protect Lorielle.

But of course she hadn't been a cop then. And now he worried that one day she wouldn't be able to protect herself.

"All right, it's time for show-and-tell," Roberta announced as she opened a collection of metal boxes and extracted various plastic bags. "The first is marijuana," she said as she handed a bag of what appeared to be dried herbs to the reporter at the first table. "Some of you might recognize this, and if so, see me after class."

Uneasy chuckles emanated from the group.

"I see there'll be quite a few of you," she teased, eliciting outright laughter from the citizens and her fellow officers.

She was a natural speaker. She could be such an asset at the shelter. If only she'd quit the police department...

She lifted another plastic bag. "They look just like rocks, don't they?" Through the plastic bag, she squeezed one of the crystal-shaped pieces. "This is crack. It's smoked, instead of snorted like powder cocaine." She dropped that bag onto another table. "And black-tar heroin—yup, it's actually mixed with tar."

Marla shuddered as she passed the plastic bag to Holden. His hand trembled as he passed the bag to the person beside him. He didn't even glance at the contents; he had seen it before, in his sister's apartment the night he'd found her overdosed. The night Holly, barely old enough to remember his number, had called him for help. Even though he'd gotten there before the ambulance arrived, before his sister died, he had been too late to save her.

He expelled a shaky breath and glanced up, catching Roberta's gaze on him. There was a question in her blue eyes. He nodded. *I'm okay...*

"And these," she continued, holding out another bag, "look like candy. They're actually X—ecstasy tablets."

"They do look like candy," Bernie Gillespie exclaimed, "the kind my grandchildren are always eating." She clutched her husband's arm.

"The drug dealers package it like this to hook kids young," Roberta explained. "Then they move them on to harder drugs. Crack is highly addictive because that first high is the highest, so they keep chasing the high. Heroin—" she focused on Holden again "—is also highly addictive."

Even if she wouldn't quit the Lakewood PD, Holden needed Robbie at the shelter; he needed her to talk to his kids about drugs. It was a struggle for him to do without being overwhelmed by pain and regret and guilt.

"Hey," Ethan Brewer said to Holden as the CPA wrapped up for the evening. The sergeant had attended this class and brought along his dog, as he'd jokingly threatened, "to make sure no one tried to smuggle out the drugs Officer Meyers had brought for show-and-tell."

Now he met Holden's gaze and grinned. "You going to the Lighthouse?"

"Lighthouse?" Holden asked.

Bernie Gillespie answered for Ethan. "It's a great bar and restaurant where the police officers hang out after their shifts. Well, most of the police officers, anyway."

Holden could guess who didn't. Roberta would go home to Kayla, not hang out with her colleagues. He had been so wrong about her—she put her daughter first.

"Brigitte's grandfather owns the place," Ethan added. "They have the best burger and fries on the lakeshore."

"Thanks, we think so, too," Brigitte Kowalczek said. The pretty bartender was also a member of the Citizens'

Police Academy. "So have we piqued your interest, Reverend Thomas?"

"It's kind of late to eat," he said, and after seeing all those drugs he had no appetite.

"I'll work on him," Ethan promised, waving off the others. He waited until they walked out of the conference room before adding, "Give Meredith a call. Have her join us. Some social workers can be a pain in the ass, but we all really like her. She'd fit in well."

"Thanks," Holden said. He truly appreciated the cop's friendship. "But I'm going to have to make it another time. I have someplace else I need to be tonight." He turned to leave and bumped into *her*. "Robbie…"

"Don't let me keep you," she said as she hurried out the door.

But Holden was worried that she *would* keep him, at least keep him interested…that she was going to cause him to break his promise to Lorielle.

ROBBIE LAY in the bathtub, steam rising as the hot water eased some of her tension. Yet a bath couldn't ease all of it. She suspected only Holden could do that.

She lifted a wineglass from the white-tiled floor. Her fingers grasping the stem, she swirled the red wine. After uttering a wistful sigh, she sipped from the rim. The wine was dry and tart and spread warmth through her chest. The warmth reminded her of Holden's kisses. Despite the heat of the water, she shivered.

She couldn't think about his kisses anymore. Or about him.

But that look on his face when he'd passed along the

bag of heroin as if he hadn't wanted to even touch it...
It was a look that had drained all the color from his
tanned face and dulled the usual spark in his bright,
green-blue eyes, and the look haunted her. She'd wanted
to make sure that he was all right, so she'd waited for
him after class. But then she'd heard Brewer telling
him to call Meredith. And her shame and guilt had
rushed back.

Meredith's talking to her on the beach had only
added to Robbie's guilt, instead of absolving her. It
didn't matter that Meredith had sworn she and Holden
were only friends. It didn't matter, because Robbie had
had no business kissing him, not when he refused to
accept her as she was. And even if he could, his father
would never accept his son becoming involved with a
"dirty stray."

She blinked, her lashes fluttering. The steam—it
had to be the steam—was bringing tears to her eyes.
She did not cry.

She swallowed another mouthful of wine, nearly
choking on it as a knock sounded on the apartment
door. "Great," she muttered, debating for a moment
about just ignoring it.

But maybe Kayla had awakened in Brenda's apartment and wanted to come down to her own bed. Robbie
rose from the bubbles, quickly wrapped a towel around
herself and tucked the end between her breasts.

When she pulled open the door a moment later,
however, it wasn't her daughter who waited in the
hall. She blew out a shaky breath. She should have
ignored the knock.

"Y-you were in the tub," Holden stammered as he

stared at her bare shoulders, his pupils widening until his eyes were completely dark with desire.

"I thought you had someplace else you needed to be," she said.

"Yeah. Here." He stepped forward, pushing against the door, until he was inside. Then he closed the door behind himself so the two of them were alone in her apartment. And she was barely covered by a towel. He held out his hand, her borrowed sandals dangling from his finger. "I brought back your glass slippers."

"They don't really fit," she informed him. "They're Joelly's. She's the princess and I'm the cop."

Her blunt reminder wasn't strong enough to dampen his desire for her.

"Where is Kayla?" he asked, needing to know that the child was nearby in order to hang on to his tenuous control. Again Roberta was someone else entirely, someone soft and beautiful and vulnerable as she stared at him, her eyes wide.

"Up...upstairs."

He closed his eyes, trying to resist the temptation to touch her, to stroke his fingers over all that bare skin and follow the path of the beads of water that streaked over her breasts and disappeared beneath the towel. He shook his head, ejecting her sensual half-naked image from his mind as he tried to remember why he'd felt compelled to come here. "I—I wanted to talk to you..."

He needed to apologize, for kissing her on the beach and for the idiotic comments his father had made.

"I wanted to talk to you, too," she said, her voice husky. "That's why I waited tonight...for you."

His body tensed, desire gripping him so that every

muscle ached to hold her, to possess her. "You waited for me? Why?"

"I saw your face," she said. "I knew what you must have been going through. I'm sorry."

His gaze met hers. Her eyes were warm and full of concern. "I don't want to talk now," he said.

Her skin, already flushed from the bath, grew pinker. "What *do* you want?"

He reached out, hooking his fingers over the top of her towel between the curves of her breasts. "You."

Her lips parted, her breath shuddering out. "Holden…"

"Stop me," he almost pleaded. Every time he saw her, touched her, tasted her, it was harder for him to remember his promise to Lorielle—let alone keep it. "Please, stop me."

She wrapped her fingers around his, pulling them away from her towel. Then she dropped his hand and stepped back.

He should have been relieved that she had the control he lacked. But the sharp bite of disappointment added to the ache of desire. "Yeah, you're right. We can't do this," he said, his lungs straining for breath as he stared at her.

She was so damn beautiful, her blue eyes wide and heavily lashed in her delicate face. Her silky black hair curled wildly around her bare shoulders. And the damp towel clung to every curve of her body.

Then she lifted her hand to where she'd tucked the end of the towel between her breasts and tugged the end free. The towel slid down her body, leaving every sweet, sexy inch of her bare.

A groan ripped from his throat. "Roberta…"

Paralyzed with desire, he couldn't move as she walked past him, close enough that she just brushed his tense, aching body. She turned back and crooked her finger.

Before he got any closer, close enough to touch, he had to ask, "Are you sure?"

Chapter Twelve

What the hell am I doing? Robbie shivered, not from the cold but from the way Holden looked at her—as if he could not look away. And she couldn't walk away, not without him.

"Roberta, are you sure?" he asked again.

She should have realized it wasn't Kayla at the door—Brenda had confessed that the little girl had stayed awake past her bedtime. She would be out cold for the rest of the night. But Robbie didn't intend to be alone while her daughter slept upstairs.

"I'm sure," she said.

Holden released a ragged breath and closed the distance between them. "That makes one of us."

She entwined her fingers with his and tugged him into her bedroom. Then she closed and locked the door behind them. "I think we need to do this," she said, "so we can put it—and each other—behind us."

"I'm not going to use you like that," he protested, ever the gentleman. His conflict was apparent in the twitch of muscles along his jaw.

"No," she agreed, "I'm going to use you." She would

use his kisses and his touch to release the frustration he had built inside her. Once it was gone, maybe she could stop thinking and dreaming about him.

A wicked chuckle rumbled out of his chest. "I have no problem with you using me."

"So you don't mind being used," she said. Some of the teens that came through his shelter took advantage of him, of his generosity and his desire to save them. Tonight she wanted that desire only for her.

"I don't mind *you* using me," he clarified, squeezing her fingers. Then he lifted his free hand and traced the curve of her cheek. "You are so beautiful...and so tough."

His tribute to her toughness was the compliment that had her blinking back tears. Seeing that he knew how much her strength mattered to her convinced Robbie she was doing the right thing. Even if they had no future together, even if she wasn't the kind of woman he could marry, she wanted to make love with Holden. She wanted this night to remember.

"Holden..." She swallowed hard, desire thick in her throat. "Undress for me."

His mouth quirked into a grin. "For a minute I thought you said *arrest*—that you were arresting me again."

"I might get out the cuffs," she threatened playfully, "if you don't do what I want."

He stepped back, then shrugged off his jacket. Next he reached for the hem of his charcoal-gray sweater and pulled it over his head, muscles rippling on his washboard abs as he dropped it on the floor.

Robbie's fingers itched to touch him as desire overwhelmed her. He was male perfection. So damned good-looking she suspected most of those teenage girls stayed at his shelter just to stare at him. *Her* mouth hung open in awe of his masculine beauty.

He unclasped his belt and pulled it free of his jeans, then unsnapped and unzipped the denim. The open fly revealed his boxers, which had a cartoon cat on them. When he noticed that she was smiling he said with a laugh, "Holly picked them out for me."

"She has great taste," Robbie replied, and reached out, pushing the denim down his lean hips. He stepped out of his shoes and kicked off his jeans, leaving on only those boxers.

"I like your taste," he said, but he didn't even glance around at her lavender-and-slate-gray bedroom. Instead, he tangled his fingers in her hair and held her head steady as he covered his mouth with hers. His tongue parted her lips, then slid in and out as he tasted her.

She kissed him back with all the fire burning inside her. Their bodies just touched, her breasts rubbing his chest. She shivered at the erotic sensation of the soft, golden brown hair against her skin.

He scooped her up and carried her to the bed. She wanted his lips again. She arched into him and wrapped her arms around his waist, pulling his weight down onto her. His erection strained against his boxers, long and hard, and pressed into her stomach.

Easing his mouth from hers, his breath hot against her throat, he slid his lips down her neck. She flung her head back, then glided her hands up his back, tunneling her fingers into his hair and pulling him closer. He kissed her shoulder before his lips traced the curve of her breast. Finally he touched the aching point with the tip of his tongue.

She gasped. "Holden…"

He continued to tease her, using just his tongue while his fingers skimmed along her sides to the curve of her hips. Finally he tugged her nipple fully into his mouth, scraping the sensitive tip with his teeth. While one hand cupped her other breast, the fingers of his free hand skimmed over her stomach to tangle in the curls between her legs. He stroked through them to slide first one finger inside her, then another, while his thumb teased the most sensitive part of her. The tension built inside her, making her muscles contract until finally she shuddered and came.

"Holden!"

"I have to taste you," he said, but instead of kissing her lips, he moved down her body and slipped his tongue inside her. He stroked it in and out, just as his fingers had done.

Robbie clutched at his shoulders, then laced her fingers through his hair. "I want you. Now!"

"If I don't do what you say, will you arrest me?" he teased.

"I will get out the cuffs," she warned.

He stood up and shoved his boxers down his hips. Then he grabbed his jeans, rooted in a pocket and pulled out a condom. After rolling it on, he knelt between her legs. The tip of his penis nudged through her curls, then pushed against her.

She arched her hips and stretched as he thrust deep. Biting her lip, she held back a moan at the sensation of

Holden buried inside her. Then he pulled out, just a bit, before thrusting deep again.

He groaned. "You feel so…"

Right. It felt right making love with him.

He leaned down and kissed her, imitating with his tongue in her mouth what was going on below, stroking in and out. She locked her legs around his waist, pulling him deeper yet. Her nails gently raked his back as the tension grew inside her.

Then he reached between them and touched that sensitive nub again. A scream burned in her throat as she came again, shuddering beneath him. With one more deep thrust, he buried his face against her neck and uttered a primal growl. At last he collapsed on her, then rolled onto his back, his chest rising and falling as he panted for breath.

Robbie fought to breathe, too, and to recover the control she'd lost in his arms. She was afraid that her control wasn't all she'd lost. Had Holden taken her heart, as well?

When he slipped from the bed, she sighed—was it relief or did she feel bereft? But he returned moments later, crawling in beside her. His voice still rough with desire, he murmured, "That was…"

A mistake.

"I know," she assured him.

"…amazing," he said with a ragged sigh as he wrapped his arms around her.

Helpless to resist, Robbie curled against him and laid her cheek on his chest where his heart was beating hard. "It was…" So much more than she had expected. More than she had feared it would be.

"I didn't come over here for that," he said.

"You came to talk," she said, remembering. "About what?"

"I came to apologize," Holden said as he stroked his fingers over her bare shoulder, "for kissing you on the beach."

She laughed. "We just did a little more than kissing. It's okay. Meredith assured me you aren't a cheating bastard."

"Just a bastard," he remarked with a faint trace of amusement. "I think I get that from my father. I'm really sorry about what he said."

She settled her cheek against his chest. "You don't need to apologize. It's not like what he said isn't the truth. I was a stray that Joelly dragged home."

"That's how you got off the streets?"

She nodded. She hated talking about her past, hated thinking about what could have happened to her and her daughter. "You listen to people's problems all day. You don't need all the gory details of my past." He wouldn't appreciate some of the things he might learn about her.

"You've told me bits and pieces, Robbie," he said, his fingers playing with her hair now, "but I'd like the details. Starting from the beginning."

She sighed. Sharing her past was sharing too much of herself; it was more intimate than making love with him.

"Tell me," he urged her.

She shook her head, unwilling to give any more of herself to a man who'd once vowed he would never love her.

"Robbie, I *need* to know."

And maybe she needed to tell him.

She'd once been such a fool; she hated admitting it. "I warned you. You've heard it before. Teenage girl falls in love with teenage boy. Thinks he's the one. Romeo to her Juliet." She forced a short laugh. "They really shouldn't make kids read that in English lit."

"Yeah," he agreed, "teenagers tend to overlook how that story ended."

"Our story ended when I got pregnant. Romeo wanted me to get rid of *it*." Anger surged through her again as she remembered how Kayla's father had referred to his unborn child. "So that *it* wouldn't mess up his football scholarship. I already told you that Romeo wasn't the only one who wanted me to get rid of *it*."

He blew out a breath that stirred her hair. "Your parents did, too."

"They were insistent." Her heart clutched with re-membered pain and fear. "I was so scared to tell them—so scared I had disappointed them."

"But they disappointed *you*."

So much so that when she'd gotten busted she had not been able to make her one phone call home to them. She'd had no one to call in the way that Joelly had called her father. "Yes."

"So you ran away to protect Kayla."

She fisted her hand on his chest. "I was so stupid. Trying to save her, I could have gotten us both killed. I probably would have if I hadn't met Joelly."

"You really need to share your story with more people," he said.

"You want me to talk to the TV networks or the *Chronicle?*" She laughed. "I hardly think they would be interested." Even her own parents hadn't been interested in what had happened to her—or their grandchild.

"The kids at the shelter would be interested in how you went from living on the streets to patrolling them. How did that happen, Robbie?" His voice was rough with emotion. "How did you get off the streets?"

When Lorielle hadn't, he no doubt thought.

Robbie wrapped both arms around him, holding him tight, offering comfort. But he remained tense with the same pain and guilt tonight's class had apparently brought back for him.

"So tell me," he persisted, "how'd you do it?"

This was the part she hadn't wanted to tell him, but she couldn't continue to ignore his question. "I got *arrested*."

"You have a record?" he asked in surprise.

She shook her head. "My charges were dropped because Joelly claimed all the drugs were hers when they booked us."

"Were they?" he asked, his voice barely above a whisper.

She couldn't lie to him. "No."

"You were pregnant…"

"I wasn't using them," she said. "I was selling them. We were desperate. We had to do something to survive. It was either sell drugs or sell ourselves…" She slid a hand down her face, trying to wipe away the shame. "To our credit, it was our first sale. Our customer was a cop."

"One of Lakewood's finest?"

She smiled. "The finest. Chief Archer himself. That was over nine years ago—he was a captain then."

"But he was working undercover?"

"He was training someone." Someone who had died in the line of duty a year later, but she wasn't going to share that with Holden. He already thought her job too dangerous. "He also may have been looking for Joelly at her father's request. He got us off the streets.

"Joelly finally called her dad, and the chief took us to the mayor's house." Emotion rushed over her, cracking her voice as she added, "I will never forget the look on Joel Standish's face."

Holden must have picked up on her wistfulness, for he patted her back as if she needed comforting. She didn't need it now, but she was going to need it when he left.

"It wasn't like your father said," she insisted with pride, "that I was a dirty stray who'd followed her home."

"My father's an ass," he responded, his voice hard with bitterness. "He's the reason Lorielle ran away. After he divorced her mother, his only contact with Lorielle was the checks he sent. And he has no contact with Holly."

"I'm sorry," she said. "She deserves better."

"She really likes you."

"I like her." The truth was, she was falling for the child. "She's a sweet girl."

"Quit your job," Holden said. "You could do so much more at the shelter because you really understand."

If only he understood *her.*

"Because I've been where they are," she replied, "I know all the pretty speeches and lectures in the world aren't going to help them. They're not going to listen."

Color flushed his face. "So I'm wasting my time?"

"I didn't say that."

"But you think it."

"Joelly and I have talked about how we wished you'd been around back when we were on the streets. We would have loved having a safe place to sleep, a warm meal…" She pressed a kiss to his chest. "You're doing a good thing," she assured him. "Really, you are."

"But I'm not doing enough," he said with a resigned sigh. "And it's only safe now because of your visit. You did so much in that one visit. If you worked there every day you could help these kids a lot, Robbie."

"I help them more by being a cop," she said, "by getting the dealers and the johns and other criminals off the street." She pulled away from him, but she suspected it was too late, that she'd already fallen for him. "And now I have to put you on the street."

"What?"

"You have to leave," she said. "You can't be here when Kayla comes home. I can't have her getting the wrong idea."

A grin curved his lips. "Yeah, Mrs. Groom called. They're already telling everyone that they're sisters."

"You think it's funny that they're lying?" she asked with concern. Honesty was very important to her.

His grin faded. "No, of course not."

"It's bad enough that they're confusing their classmates and teacher. We don't need to confuse them, too. You need to leave before Kayla sees you. I don't want her getting the wrong idea."

"Is it the wrong idea?" he asked.

"I think we both know it is." If only her heart would realize it. "I can never be that woman you promised your sister you would find for Holly."

"Robbie, I wish—"

She shook her head. "I can't change who or what I am." Not even for the man she loved.

"SOMETIMES I FORGET what she looked like," Holly said as she climbed into Holden's lap and took her mother's picture from his hands. "She was so pretty."

"Like you," he said, tickling her under the chin. She squirmed and giggled and tried to tickle him back. The chair rolled farther back from his desk in the den.

After a few gasps for breath, her laughter subsided and she stared at the picture Holden had taken of her mother just a few months after she'd given birth to Holly. Lorielle's gaze was warm with love and respect. She had idolized her big brother. But he'd let her down; he hadn't been able to help her.

"Mom would have liked Miss Meyers," Holly said. "I bet they would have been friends, like her and Miss Jo are."

Maybe...when they'd been kids. But Lorielle wouldn't have liked Roberta for Holly. She would not have wanted a woman who put her life at risk every time she clocked in for a shift as her daughter's new mother. She wouldn't want her child to suffer through any more of the uncertainty that Holly had already suffered through having a drug addict for a mother.

Holly tipped back her head to meet his gaze. "Do you like Miss Meyers?"

Holden more than liked her. He was afraid he was falling in love with her.

"What do you remember about your mother?" he asked the child.

She was quiet and still—and Holly was never quiet

and still. Finally she released a shaky breath. "I remember that she didn't look this pretty. She usually had really dark circles around her eyes, sometimes bruises. Sometimes her lip would bleed. I remember her leaving me home alone."

"I'm sorry, honey," he said, hugging her close. He shouldn't have brought up Lorielle. But he hadn't realized that Holly would remember so much.

He didn't think of Lorielle now. He thought, instead, of Robbie's bruises and blood. He couldn't put Holly through that pain and uncertainty again— not even for Roberta.

ROBBIE STARED at her friend's face until Joelly sensed her presence and opened her eyes. The blonde jumped, knocking her blankets from her shoulders. "What the hell!"

Sassy, sleeping on a cushion beside the bed, yipped.

"A little late to warn me now," Joelly told her watchdog as she rubbed her eyes and scooted up against the pillows piled on her bed. "Did I leave the door unlocked or did you use your key?"

"Key," Robbie said. "Just like you used mine to surprise me a few weeks ago."

"At least I brought you coffee."

"I brought you shoes," Robbie said, dropping the heels on the floor near Joelly's overflowing closet.

Jo's brow furrowed in confusion. "I thought you lost them."

"Someone found them for me."

Jo emitted a squeal of delight, which had Sassy barking. "Your very own Prince Charming."

Robbie shook her head. "I don't want a prince. Or any other man right now," she said with a glare.

"Uh-oh, you have that look," her friend observed with an exaggerated shiver. "What did I do?"

"Don't help me."

"What do you mean?" Joelly widened her eyes into the blank stare she used to convince people she was an empty-headed ditz. Joelly perpetuated all the myths about herself because she was afraid of anyone getting to know her and rejecting her in the way she felt her father had rejected her. But sometimes she just used those myths for her own amusement.

Because Robbie knew how smart Joelly really was, the ditzy look always infuriated her. "You know what I'm talking about."

She would have confronted her friend earlier about her machinations, but she hadn't had a chance to catch her alone. And Robbie hadn't wanted to have this conversation in front of Kayla.

"No, I don't," Joelly said, her eyes still wide with feigned innocence.

"You know," Robbie prodded her. "You had your dad invite Holden to the ball."

Jo grimaced and mumbled, "You'd think a politician would know how to keep a secret."

"Stop trying to throw us together," Robbie warned her. "I know what you're up to, and I don't appreciate your matchmaking. I don't need a love life."

"Why not?" Joelly asked. "One of us should have one."

"Not me. I have a daughter to worry about," Robbie reminded her. "I don't need a man who disapproves of what I am."

"What do you mean?"

"He doesn't think I should be a cop."

"Then he doesn't understand you at all," Joelly said. "I'm sorry…"

Tears stung Robbie's eyes now. "Not as sorry as I am."

Joelly patted the bed next to her, and Sassy jumped onto her lap. But she patted again, and Robbie crawled in beside her just as she had when they were kids and as Joelly had done with her just a few weeks ago. They'd always been more like sisters than friends. Jo slid her arm around Robbie's shoulders. "Well, at least you got everything out in the open and found out it wasn't going to work before things went too far between the two of you."

Robbie crooked her neck until her head settled against Joelly's shoulder and she released a miserable sigh. "Too late."

"Oh, Robbie…" Joelly stroked a hand over her hair in the same way she stroked her dog's fur. "What happened?"

"We made love," she admitted.

"Then it did go too far for you. You love him."

Robbie sucked in a breath. "No. I don't," she lied, to her best friend and herself. "I don't have to be in love to make love. As we both know, I'm not the virgin. You are."

"You would be, too, if the only guys who showed any interest in you were really just after your father's money and connections."

A twinge of sympathy struck Robbie's heart. She understood the fear of rejection and thinking that you weren't good enough. But Joelly had no reason to have low self-esteem. "Jo, that's not true. You have more to offer than you realize. They're attracted to you, not your father's money."

"That hasn't been the case in the past."

"You dated some losers," Robbie admitted. "But there are good guys out there. You need to keep looking."

As usual Jo moved the focus away from her own love life. "I really believed Holden Thomas was one of them."

"He is a good guy," Robbie agreed. "He's just not the guy for me." He would have been, had he been able to accept her as she was.

"The guy for you is out there," Joelly said, then wistfully continued, "The guy who will appreciate you and everything that you are…you'll find him. You just have to keep looking."

"No, there's no reason for me to look." Robbie doubted she'd ever find someone who'd accept her as she was. "I don't want or need a man in my life." She held her friend's gaze and insisted, "I don't need a love life."

Joelly held up her hands. "I understand. No more matchmaking."

"Promise?"

"Promise. But I'm not the only matchmaker you need to worry about," Joelly reminded her.

Robbie sighed and dropped her head back onto Joelly's shoulder. "My daughter."

"Kayla has her heart set on you and *Uncle* Holden getting together."

How Robbie had hoped that her daughter would never have to experience what she had years ago and was experiencing again now. Heartbreak.

Chapter Thirteen

Kayla's tummy ached, but it wasn't because she'd eaten too much pizza. She'd barely finished a slice. And it wasn't because she'd picked up some bug from school, although there'd been a lot of kids out sick this past week.

Holly must have felt sick, too, because she just lay beside Kayla on the living-room floor. Their favorite cartoon played across the television screen, but Kayla really didn't see it.

"What's up, you two?" her mom asked from the chair she was curled up in. "You're both so quiet. You're not fighting, are you?"

Holly glanced at Kayla, then guiltily looked away.

"It's not your fault," she told her friend.

"What's not Holly's fault?" her mom asked. She dropped onto the floor next to them. "What's going on?"

Tears filled Holly's eyes, then spilled over onto her cheeks. "I'm so sorry that Uncle Holden took someone else to that stupid ball."

Mom smiled, but somehow it looked a little sad, as if only her lips were moving. "Of course your uncle would take someone else. He and I aren't dating. And you should give Meredith a chance. She's a very nice woman."

"B-but she's not you," Holly wailed, throwing her arms around Mom's neck.

Kayla winced, knowing that her mom's neck had been hurt a few weeks ago. It looked better now, just kind of yellow, and she'd stopped wearing the scarves. She hated it when her mom got hurt, but it was part of her job. And like Aunt JoJo always said, Mom was so much tougher than any bad guy.

"B-but we wanted you two to get married," Holly confessed between sniffles.

"Oh, sweetheart," her mom said as she patted Holly's back, "I'm sorry, but that's not going to happen."

"B-but I want *you* to be my mom," Holly said, her voice squeaky from crying.

Mom hugged Holly tighter, the way she always hugged Kayla, as if she was never going to let her go. "I don't have to be married to your uncle for us to be close," she said.

"You don't?"

"Nope. Aunt JoJo's dad is like my dad, even though my mom never married him," she explained. "He still does nice things for me and spends time with me."

"He does?"

Mom nodded. "Yes. And since you and Kayla are best friends, I'll be spending a lot of time with you."

But not if Uncle Holden was around, Kayla bet. Mrs. Crayden had dropped Holly off here, and last weekend Aunt JoJo had been in charge of dropping her off and picking her up from Uncle Holden's house.

"You're already very special to me, and that will never change," Mom promised Holly.

"Even if my uncle marries this other woman?"

Mom's expression changed and her face turned pale. "Even if."

EXCEPT FOR THE KARAOKE machine, the noise in the Lighthouse Bar & Grill reminded Holden of the shelter—voices raised in conversation and smatterings of laughter. Here, there was also the aroma of good food, but even the scent of grilling burgers couldn't tempt Holden to eat. Since the night Robbie had kicked him out of her bed a couple of weeks ago, he had lost his appetite.

Baskets of fries and sticky chicken wings and deep-fried zucchini sticks and mushrooms covered the long table where most of the CPA sat. But Holden shook his head when Marla Halliday held out one of the baskets of food.

A strong hand slapped his shoulder. "Great to see you, Holden. I'm glad you stopped by to join the rest of the group after class."

After seeing Roberta at tonight's session—it was the first time since they'd made love—Holden hadn't trusted himself to go home and not head for her place, instead. He forced a smile for the watch commander. "I'm glad to be here, Lieutenant O'Donnell."

Patrick laughed as if he'd seen right through his lie. "Just watch out for Bernie. She'll try to talk you into singing."

"He wants to sing?" the older woman asked, gesturing for Holden to follow her toward the game area.

He shook his head. "Karaoke is not for me. I only sing in church." And sometimes there Holly mocked him for being off-key.

The lieutenant asked, "So are you enjoying the Citizens' Police Academy?"

He nodded. "Yes, I'm learning a lot. Your brother was really informative tonight." The Special Response Team sergeant had been very open about what his unit had to deal with and about the difficult choices he'd had to make in order to save innocent lives.

Patrick O'Donnell glanced toward the bar, where his younger brother was tossing back a shot glass of liquor. "Maybe a little too informative."

"Doing what he does…" Holden shook his head. Sean O'Donnell didn't put just his life in danger, but also his soul.

"Yeah, it's tough." The watch commander sighed, his face tight with concern for his brother. "So is your work down at the shelter, though. Trying to help those kids can't be easy."

"No," Holden admitted. "They're distrustful and cynical." And as Roberta had discovered in the back alley, they were dangerous. "I appreciate the police visits."

"Even Officer Meyers's?" O'Donnell asked with a grin.

"Yeah, she pointed out some necessary changes and the shelter's much safer now. And the kids love when Sergeant Brewer and his partner visit."

Ethan dropped into the empty chair next to his. "They love Jaws. I'm just his chauffeur. Too bad we didn't have more free time to come by."

"I understand now how overworked you guys are," Holden told them. "I appreciate whatever time you can give to the shelter."

"I'd like to have you and Rafe Sanchez speak during

the community-involvement class," Patrick said. "It would be great if you two could explain your programs."

Holden nodded. "We'd be honored." And he was interested in learning how Rafe Sanchez had gone from gang member to the philanthropist who'd started an after-school program...for kids at risk of joining gangs.

Patrick grabbed his ringing cell phone from his belt and read the ID screen. "This is important. I have to go." He glanced at the bar again, then turned back to Ethan. "Can you keep an eye on my little bro for me?"

"Sure thing," Brewer promised. "Don't worry about him."

Patrick nodded, but Holden doubted it was because he wouldn't worry anymore. It was impossible not to worry about a younger sibling you knew was struggling with demons. But Holden didn't blame the SRT sergeant for having a drink, not after what he'd shared in class about his job.

"So tell me," Ethan said, turning back to Holden once his boss had left, "is the gorgeous Meredith joining you tonight?"

"No."

"You're still seeing her, though," Ethan said as if Holden would be crazy to do otherwise.

"Yes." They had just talked about one of the kids at the shelter and about Holly. He'd like her to spend some time with his niece. While Merry would probably never become the mother Lorielle had made him promise to find for her daughter, she could become a positive female role model. So that Holly would stop gushing about Robbie.

Hearing a slight gasp, he glanced up and met Roberta's gaze. She had joined the CPA group at the long table. Had she followed him from class? No, from the look of shock on her face, she hadn't expected to see him. That was probably the only reason she'd come along.

"That's great," Ethan continued. "Meredith's perfect for you."

Robbie's chair made a scraping sound as she shoved it back and jumped to her feet. "I'm going to get a drink from the bar. You two need anything?"

Ethan lifted a water bottle. "I'm set. You, Holden? Do you need anything?"

Her. He needed Robbie. But he shook his head and let her walk away.

"So when are you going out with her again?" Ethan asked.

"We never went out," Holden said, realizing it was true. He had kissed her and made love with her, but he had never taken her out on a date. Despite her claim that he hadn't used her, he felt as if he had—and he felt like scum because of it.

"I wasn't talking about Robbie," Ethan said with a chuckle, which trailed off as he studied Holden's face. "Oh, God."

He sighed and admitted, "Yeah…"

"You're in love with Robbie."

Holden opened his mouth to deny it, but the words wouldn't come out. He *was* in love with her.

"WHAT CAN I get you, Officer Meyers?" Brigitte Kowalczek asked from behind the bar.

Since she couldn't have what she really wanted, a relationship with Holden Thomas, Roberta thought about settling for a drink. A strong drink.

"Decaf coffee," she ordered, instead. Kayla was already asleep, upstairs in Brenda's apartment. She didn't need her mother tonight. Robbie realized now that she sometimes used her daughter as an excuse to stay home. Maybe, like Joelly, she was afraid of rejection. Of course, Holden had proved she had good reason to be afraid.

"What about you, Reverend Thomas?" Brigitte asked.

Robbie's back tingled as she realized he stood right behind her. And her heart ached, knowing that even though he stood so close, he would never be hers.

"I'm good," he told the bartender. "I don't need anything."

After Brigitte handed her a mug of steaming coffee, Robbie turned toward Holden. "If you don't need anything, why'd you follow me to the bar?"

"Because I need to apologize to you," he said, his handsome face tight with concern and guilt. "I'm sorry…"

"About still seeing Meredith?" she asked, and waved a hand dismissively. "She told me that the two of you are just friends. But Brewer's right. She is perfect for you—and Holly."

"Holly doesn't think so," he said with a heavy sigh.

"I'm sure she'll come around," Robbie said, nearly choking on her jealousy.

"Meredith's not perfect."

"She's pretty damn close to it," Robbie said.

"But she's not you."

"You don't want me," she reminded him.

"Robbie—"

"Robbie!" someone else shouted her name. Then Sean O'Donnell slid his arm around her shoulders. "Oh, hey, Reverend…" He glanced from one to the other of them. "I'm not interrupting something here, am I?"

"No," Robbie assured him. "Not a thing." She turned toward the SRT sergeant, but she noticed from the corner of her eye when Holden slipped away.

"It would never work," Sean told her.

"What?"

"You and the reverend," he said. "Only a cop can truly understand a cop." His arm tightened around her shoulders. "*I* could understand you."

"I understand you, too," Robbie said. Even though she hadn't been needed at the CPA tonight, she had ducked into the back of the room to hear Sean speak. Like his brother, this O'Donnell was also a legend in Lakewood. A former Special Ops sniper, he was the go-to guy for the SRT. After the things he'd revealed about his job tonight, Robbie had suspected he might need some support. That was why she'd come to the Light-house. "Why don't I give you a ride home?"

He sighed and nodded. "Sounds great." He kept his arm around her shoulders as they walked toward the door.

Just before they passed through it, Robbie turned back and caught Holden's gaze. She knew what he thought—that she was going home with Sean to spite him for still seeing Meredith. But really she was only taking care of a fellow officer.

"Your car-r-r is pink," Sean murmured with a laugh as he slid into the passenger's seat of Joelly's SUV. "I wouldn't have figured you for a pink car."

"It's not mine," she said and then asked, "Are you staying with your brother yet?"

He shook his head. "N-no, I have my own place now." But he slurred the directions to it so badly, she still wasn't sure she had the right complex when she pulled into the lot.

"Is this it?"

He peered through the windshield for several long seconds as if trying to clear his vision, then finally nodded.

"It looks like a nice place."

"It would be," he grumbled, "if n-n-not for my neighbor."

"I'm lucky," she said, "my neighbor is my best friend."

"My neighbor hates my guts," he said as he opened the passenger door and stepped onto the asphalt of the parking lot. He stumbled back, rocking the SUV as he fell against the side of the vehicle. "Wanna come up with me?"

In addition to being the best shot in the department, Sean O'Donnell was also the biggest playboy. Of course he was probably too drunk right now to make a pass at her. And despite his size and reputation, there was a vulnerability to him tonight that struck a chord within her.

"I'll be a gentleman," she teased, "and show you to your door."

His infamous grin flashed. "*I* can't promise to be a gentleman."

"I'd know you were lying if you tried," she said.

He threw his arm around her shoulders again and they climbed the stairs to his third-floor apartment. As he fumbled his key into his door, he asked, "How come you and I never…?" He waggled his brows. "Is it because you have a kid?"

"Kayla."

"That's a pretty name. I bet she's a pretty kid, too, if she looks like her mom," he said with the kind of offhand charm that had earned him his reputation. That and all his many, many conquests. "You're r-really pretty, Robbie…"

The door next to his opened, and a familiar face peeked through the crack. "Oh…"

"Miss Gorman, right?" Robbie asked, recognizing the teacher who was attending the CPA. Was she the neighbor who hated Sean?

The woman nodded. "I'm sorry. I thought someone was at my door." But her gaze locked onto Sean until he turned toward her. Then she murmured a good-night and slammed her door shut.

"Yup, she hates me," Sean murmured.

"But why?" If not for the SRT sergeant, Miss Gorman probably would have died a few years ago when her class had been taken hostage.

"She's not a cop," Sean said as if that explained everything. "She doesn't understand—" his throat moved as he swallowed hard "—that I had to…that I had no choice…"

While sympathy for Sean gripped her, Robbie breathed an inward sigh of relief that she had never had to take a life, as he had in order to save the hostages. She'd had a few close scrapes, two of the closest just since meeting Holden, but she'd never had to make the decisions that Sean had.

"You had no choice," she agreed. "Or the guy would have killed his teacher and classmates."

"S-see, you're a cop," he said, "you understand."

Apparently Ms. Gorman believed her troubled student hadn't had to die.

"You really believe that cops should only be with cops?"

"It sure would save a lot of hurt and confusion," he said with an insight that caught her by surprise.

Thinking of the hurt and confusion that Holden caused her, she nodded. "You're right."

"So you're coming in," he said with a wink as he finally opened his door.

She pulled his head down, but kissed only his cheek. "Good night, Sean."

Even if she was tempted, she wouldn't risk getting her heart broken again.

LEAVES FLUTTERED down from the trees lining the street on which Roberta lived. The wind whipped in off the lake, cold and brisk, sending the fallen leaves skittering across the pavement and the sidewalk where Holden paced as he waited for her.

Would she spend the night with the young sergeant? Everyone who'd seen them leave together had thought so. Ethan had whistled with surprise as they'd walked out together, the sergeant's arm around her slender shoulders.

Holden's hands tightened into fists. He should have stopped her. He should have asked her to go home with him, instead. But he had told her so many times that they had no future. Of course she would have no future with a playboy like Sean O'Donnell, either.

The thought of Robbie with the sergeant, of her making love with him as she had with Holden, had his stomach tied in knots. Anger pulsed through him so fiercely that he trembled with it.

Hell, he was acting like some damn, jealous kid, waiting outside her house for her to come home. He had just turned to his vehicle, which was parked at the curb, clicking open the locks, when lights shone on him and the trees as a car approached. It slowed, then pulled to the curb in front of his car.

Several moments passed before the door opened and Roberta stepped out. "What are you doing here?" she asked.

He waited until she joined him on the sidewalk and then he grabbed her, jerking her body against his. And he kissed her.

Chapter Fourteen

Robbie tasted jealousy in the intensity of his kiss. His lips parted hers, his tongue dipping into her mouth and stroking hers. She gripped his shoulders and shoved him back so she could breathe. "What are you doing here?" she repeated, between pants.

He shook his head. "I—I don't know."

"You don't want me."

He groaned. "We both know that's not true."

"I'm not perfect." Not like Meredith Wallingford.

"I think you're perfect," he said. "You're beautiful and smart and tough."

With each compliment, she fell deeper in love with him. "I'm a cop, too," she reminded him. "And I won't quit my job." Not even for him.

"Shh," he said. "Let's forget who and what we are tonight. Let's just be lovers."

She should send him away. She had already had her one time with him. She'd already made her memory. And yet she could always use one more…memory. "Okay."

His eyes gleamed in the faint light of the street lamps. "Is Kayla at the sitter's again?"

She nodded. Then she slid her hand into his and led him toward the front door of her apartment. With her free hand, she unlocked first that door and then her apartment door. She didn't bother flipping on a light as she tugged him toward her bedroom.

She knew she was making a mistake. That this wouldn't be just one more memory. If his compliments alone made her fall harder for him, making love with him pulled her in so deep that she would never get over him. "We shouldn't do this…"

She was right. Holden knew it, but he couldn't deny himself another night with her. "When you walked out of the bar with that SWAT guy—" jealousy rose again, grabbing him by the throat "—all I could think was that you're mine."

She shook her head. "No, I'm not. I don't belong to anyone."

"I know that," he said. "Logically I know that, but emotionally…" she belonged to him.

"We shouldn't do this again," she said as she gestured toward her bed.

Moonlight poured through the tall window, illuminating the room. And her face. Her eyes dark with desire and her skin flushed with passion, Robbie obviously wanted Holden as badly as he wanted her. So he reached for her and pulled her into his arms. "You're right."

He kissed her on the mouth. Her lips clung and her fingers caressed the hair at his nape. "It's a mistake," she murmured.

"A terrible mistake…" He couldn't stop thinking about her, couldn't stop wanting her. He would have liked to think he just needed to get her out of his system and that making love with her again would do that. But he knew better. Making love with her the first time had just made him want her more.

He fumbled with the buttons at the front of her wool blazer. As the other officers had done, Robbie had changed into her street clothes after class. She wore jeans with the jacket, and underneath the jacket, which he pushed from her shoulders, she wore only a thin lace camisole. The sight of her full breasts straining against the material kicked his temperature up a notch. He had on too many clothes, as well. He shrugged off his jacket and pulled his shirt over his head.

Soft lips touched his chest, gliding across the muscles. "You're so…so…damn good-looking," she murmured against his skin.

"And you're beautiful." He skimmed his hands over her bare shoulders, then down her sides to the hem of her camisole, which he pulled up, revealing more lace in her flimsy bra. When he unclasped the bra and pulled it from her body, moonlight washed her pale skin with a golden glow. He groaned his appreciation.

She touched him, stroking her fingers over his fly before she unsnapped his jeans and lowered the zipper. His heart slammed against his ribs when she touched him, her fingers dipping inside the waistband of his boxers.

"If you keep touching me like that, this is going to go real fast," he warned her. "And I want to take my time with you."

She shivered, as if anticipating his touch, and her fingers tightened around him. "Holden…"

He kissed her again, sliding his tongue into her

mouth as he cupped her breasts in his palms. He stroked his thumbs across the pebbled nipples.

She continued to tease him with her fingers, sliding them up and down the length of his shaft until he jerked away from her. His control snapping, he picked her up in his arms and carried her to the bed. Then he unsnapped and unzipped her jeans and eased them down her legs. He made love to her with his mouth, kissing every inch of her sweet skin, taking his time as he'd promised. He kissed the curves of her breasts before closing his lips around one of her nipples. Gently he tugged at it and then flicked his tongue over the point. To be fair, he gave equal attention to her other breast. Then he moved down her body.

She bucked when he thrust his tongue into her, and her fingers tangled in his hair, first pulling him away and then clasping him close. "Holden..."

But he didn't stop, not until she bucked again and moaned his name. Hot, sweet passion flowed over his tongue. He lapped it up, savoring the taste of her. Then he stood, his legs shaking, and kicked off his own jeans and boxers. Moments later, after donning a condom, he thrust inside the moist heat of her body. Her inner muscles gripped him, stroking as he rhythmically moved in and out.

He slid his hands between them, combing through her damp curls until he found the core of her femininity. As he rubbed, she convulsed and shuddered. His body tensed, and then his control snapped again as desire spiraled and exploded.

"Robbie!" He wanted to say more. The words *I love you* were there to be said, but he suppressed them. He couldn't give her his heart—not without breaking his promise to Lorielle and losing his integrity. But just because he didn't say the words didn't mean he didn't feel them.

He loved her.

"ARE YOU GOING to throw me out again?" he asked, shifting onto his side next to her.

Panting to regain her breath and slow her racing heart, Robbie nodded. "I have to, before Kayla comes down from Brenda's."

Holden didn't argue with her; he just rolled out of bed and began getting dressed. "You know," he murmured as he stared out the window, "we could make this work. We're two smart people. We could figure out some way to make this work for us."

This? Did he feel it, too? Did he love her as much as she loved him? Hope flared, but Robbie quickly tamped it down in favor of reality. "Let me guess. I could quit my job?"

Color flooded his face. "I wish you'd at least think about it."

She laughed, with resentment, not humor, as the SRT sergeant's words replayed through her mind. *Only a cop understands a cop.*

"Imagine working together at the shelter…"

His words doused the last of her hope. "I'm not quitting my job. And if you cared about me at all, you wouldn't ask me…"

…to change. To do what he wanted regardless of her own wants and needs. She was filled with regret and pain. He was wrong; there was no way they could make this work.

"It's because I care about you," he explained, his voice cracking with emotion, "that I want you to do something else. Your job is so dangerous."

"Do your ride-along with me," she suggested, allowing herself one last try. If she could show him that it wasn't as dangerous as he thought…

"I don't intend to do a ride-along," he said. "I've already seen enough police work, during the raid and when you arrested that guy at the shelter."

"You need to do a ride-along," she insisted. Then maybe he would finally be able to understand her job. "You'll see that most nights are really boring. Heck, it's probably more exciting to be an accountant most of the time."

"What are the exciting nights?" he asked, his voice raspy with frustration. "When you have to wrestle a drug-crazed suspect to the ground? When you get the crap beat out of you?"

"It's not like that," she said. Offended, she added, "*I'm* not like that. I'm not doing this for the thrills."

"You're doing it to keep the streets safe, but you're putting yourself in danger."

"No, what happened at the raid and the shelter, that's unusual."

"And the videos?"

"Billy pulled the worst footage for shock value," she explained. "Come on, Holden, do the ride-along. You won't be sorry." But *she* might. If something exciting did happen, it would cement his belief that marrying her would be breaking his promise to his sister.

She tensed, startled by the revelation. She wanted to marry him? Closing her eyes, she fought off the threat of tears. She couldn't lose it in front of him; he would realize how much she loved him. And her feelings would only make the situation worse for both of them.

"Robbie?"

She blinked open her eyes. "Yes?"

"Okay, I'll do it."

She waited for the sense of relief, but it didn't come. She remained tense and anxious. "That's good."

"I'll sign up for a ride-along," he agreed, "but only on one condition."

Her lips formed a smile, even though she wasn't amused. "You have conditions?"

No matter what, the man had conditions—on his love. He wouldn't give it to her unless she quit her job. She should have been used to being *loved* this way, but it had been a long time since she'd run away from home. She had nearly forgotten that feeling of utter hopelessness that had precipitated her leaving.

"Just one," he said. "I want you to do a ride-along with me first."

"Ride-along with you?" Since his condition wasn't what she expected, she laughed. "Where?"

"Just to the shelter," he said. "I need you to spend a day there."

She snorted her amusement. "Yeah, because my last visit went so well."

"At least give it a chance," he urged her. "Give us a chance."

She had no intention of quitting her job, but if spending another day at the shelter got him to take a ride-along so that he might finally accept her job…

"I'll give us a chance."

THE DINING HALL fell silent as Robbie entered. Now she understood what Joelly and the *Chronicle* reporter went through when they walked into the police station. Yet she suspected the teens' animosity toward her was even greater than the police officers' toward Jo or Erin.

"I told you this was a bad idea," she murmured to Holden, who stood beside her, his jaw taut with disapproval.

He stared at the surly teens, who were now muttering some unflattering names for her. Robbie was no stranger to those names; she'd been called them many times before. The teens hadn't appreciated her arresting someone at the shelter, and they weren't thrilled with the changes Holden had implemented because of her previous visit.

"It's gonna totally be like juvie with her here," a gangly boy grumbled.

"Cop bitch," someone else spat.

"Hey, now," Holden said, "we treat guests with respect here. And Officer Meyers is our guest."

"Miss Meyers!" squealed a little girl. Holly ran across the dining hall and flung her arms around Roberta's waist.

Robbie folded her arms around the child's shoulders, holding her close. Even before she'd found out who Holly's uncle was, she'd begun to fall for his niece. She was such a special child. "Hey, sweetheart, it's great to see you again."

The girl pulled back and peered around Roberta. "Where's Kayla?"

"With Joelly and Sassy," she said. "They were doing

manis and pedis when I left." She had been torn between staying with them on her rare Saturday off and fulfilling her side of the deal with Holden.

"Doing what?" he asked, but his eyes sparkled with amusement.

"They're painting their fingernails and toenails," Holly explained with a wistful glance at her own hands.

Mrs. Crayden seemed too no-nonsense to trouble herself with much *girl* stuff, and Holden was too masculine to play along. Poor Holly. The child really did need a mother.

"When you come over next time, we'll do our nails," Robbie promised her.

"Thanks!"

"Do you want to show Miss Meyers around?" Holden asked his niece.

Holly's head bobbed vigorously. She entwined her fingers in Robbie's and led the way around the shelter, showing her every nook and cranny of the old, four-story building that Holden must have spent hundreds of thousands converting to comfortable living quarters. They spent the longest amount of time in the arts-and-crafts room, Holly showing her some projects she'd done with the help of different teenagers.

"You're here a lot?" Robbie asked.

Holly's head bobbed again. "Yes, some days after school, but mostly on the weekends. That way I get to spend time with Uncle Holden, too."

Robbie worried that was the real reason *she* had agreed to come to the shelter—just to spend some more time with Holden. But it wouldn't matter how much time they spent together; she wasn't going to do what he wanted. She wasn't going to quit her job.

"You'd like to spend more time with him, huh?" Robbie asked.

A throat clearing drew her attention to the doorway. "Holly, Skylar's looking for you to finish your game of checkers," Holden said.

"Oh, she's a sucker for punishment." Holly tsked, sounding much older than her nine years. "I've been kicking her butt!"

"Play nice," Holden said as she sprinted past him, but Robbie was the one at whom he stared.

"Are you talking to her or me?" she asked when Holly was gone.

"You," he admitted. "Play nice with me. Give the place a chance."

He'd expected too much from her visit; he'd wanted her to fall in love with the shelter. Or maybe he'd just wanted her to fall in love with him.

"I have. I am," she insisted. "These kids don't want me here," she said with a short laugh. "They hate my guts. It wouldn't work for me to help out here. You— *they*—need someone they actually like."

"They need someone they can relate to. They need you." And he was afraid that he did, too.

"They can't relate to me if they won't listen to me."

"You didn't even try," he said.

"When should I have tried? When they were calling me names? When they were turning away from me?" She sighed. "It doesn't matter what I say—they're not going to hear me."

He hated to admit it, but she was probably right. And

he'd probably known it all along. He'd just wanted her here—with him.

"So I wasted your time?" he asked.

"It wasn't a waste of my time," she said. "I'm glad I came back. You've made some great changes here, really beefed up the security. Even though the kids resent those changes and resent me for suggesting them, you're keeping them safe. It's the perfect setup now.

"The private rooms are really nice. When Joelly and I were desperate for someplace warm to sleep, we'd go to the homeless shelter downtown, where it's all those cots set up just inches apart. It was like an army barracks. Not very private—and not safe for a couple of teenage girls."

Even though he knew she'd survived, the thought of what she'd had to endure while she was out there on the streets made tension knot at the base of his neck. "No, it wouldn't have been safe."

Lorielle had admitted that to him, too. Which was why he'd founded a shelter just for teenagers.

Robbie's blue eyes dimmed as she remembered, "We took turns sleeping."

"To watch each other's backs," Holden said. Lorielle had had no one to watch her back but him, and he hadn't been there for her.

"Sometimes we still do," she admitted. "Old habits are hard to break." She reached out and squeezed his hand. "I am impressed with what you've done. And appreciative. Lorielle would be, too."

Frustration pounded at his temples. "It's not enough."

"No," she agreed. "No matter how great this place is, it won't bring her back."

He expelled a shaky sigh. "Nothing will."

"But that still doesn't stop you from trying, from working your butt off to make it up to her." She focused on his eyes, as if trying to see into his soul. "You don't have anything to make up to her. You need to let the guilt go."

He shook his head. "I—I can't. I didn't do enough to make her quit," he admitted, his voice cracking as emotion overwhelmed him. "I didn't do enough…"

Robbie reached out and wrapped her arms around his waist, holding tight. "I know you tried." She pulled his head down and rose on tiptoe, then pressed her mouth to his, kissing him. It might have started as a kiss of comfort, but as always when they touched, passion ignited.

He tangled his fingers in her hair, holding her head still as he ravaged her mouth. Blood rushed through his body, pounding through his veins and in his ears. Maybe that was why he didn't hear the footsteps of their approach. He didn't hear anything until Skylar uttered a dramatic cry, as if she'd been wounded. And Holly clapped and giggled. Then she and the older girl whirled and rushed off.

Robbie stared at him in confusion, her eyes dazed as if she'd forgotten where they were. Then she groaned. "Now Holly saw us. I'm sure Mrs. Groom will be calling again."

"Maybe we should sit the girls down and talk to them together."

"They're a little young to hear about the birds and bees," Robbie said.

"What do you think I intended to tell them?" Holden asked in surprise.

"That it's just sex between us."

"It's not just sex," he said, although he wished it was.

She shook her head. "It can't be anything else."

"No, it can't," he agreed, because everyone would wind up getting hurt.

KAYLA RAN ACROSS the hall and grabbed the ringing telephone. "Hello?"

"Your mom's here," Holly said, her voice loud and squeaking with excitement. "At the shelter…with Uncle Holden. They're kissing again."

"Again?" Kayla heard someone in the background ask.

"Who's that?" she asked Holly.

"Skylar. She saw them, too."

Kayla heard the teenager speak again. "They've kissed before?" Skylar's voice was loud and squeaky, too, but not with excitement. She sounded mad.

"Yup," Holly answered. "My uncle's going to marry my BFF's mom."

Kayla's heart swelled as her hope grew. "And we'll be sisters."

"Yes," Holly's voice filled with satisfaction, "and I'll have a mom."

"And I'll finally have a dad."

"Hey, gotta go," Holly murmured. "Skylar's freaking out."

Her hand shook as Kayla put the phone back on the charger. When she glanced up and caught Aunt JoJo watching her from the doorway, she jumped. "Were you listening?"

Joelly nodded.

"It was Holly."

"I figured that out," Aunt JoJo said with a smile, but it was only with her mouth and not her eyes. "Don't get your hopes up, kiddo."

"But every time Mom and Uncle Holden get together, they kiss. They must really like each other. Do you think they love each other?"

"Sometimes it doesn't matter if you love each other," Aunt JoJo said.

"I don't understand." In all the fairy tales her mom had read her when Kayla was a little kid, love was all that mattered. Love was what broke all the evil spells.

"What I'm trying to say is that sometimes, no matter how much two people might love each other, they still don't belong together."

Kayla's confusion grew. "Are we talking about my mom and Holly's uncle?"

And JoJo's eyes got watery and she nodded. But Kayla had a feeling her aunt was talking about herself and some other guy. So she wrapped her arms around Aunt JoJo's skinny waist and hugged her tight.

"It'll be okay, baby," Aunt JoJo promised. But once again Kayla thought she was talking about herself, trying to convince herself everything was going to be okay.

"It will," Kayla agreed. Everything would be fine when her mom got married. She and Holly were too old to be flower girls. Would Mom let them be bridesmaids?

ROBBIE STARED at the picture on the desk in Holden's office and felt as if she was looking at an age-progression photograph of Holly. Lorielle had been a beautiful woman, much too young to die and leave behind a child.

Robbie shivered as she considered the times she herself could have died. On the streets before the mayor had taken her in…and on the streets after she became a cop. Hell, in the back alley of the shelter, if she hadn't had the strength to pull the trigger on the stun gun…

At the sound of footsteps, Robbie turned toward the door. If only she'd heard them when she and Holden were kissing…

But it was Holden this time, not the girls.

"Did you find Holly?" she asked.

"Oh, yeah."

"Did you talk to her, or are you going to wait until we can talk to Holly and Kayla together?" Yet talking to the two of them together might do more damage than good; it might give the girls the impression that they were becoming a family.

"Holly said she was *cool* with it. She *got* that we're just hanging out because we're both single and I'm not like a hundred years older than you." He pushed a hand through his hair. "Sometimes I can't believe she's only nine."

Robbie smiled and shrugged. "Maybe you should check her birth certificate."

Color drained from his face. "I don't like looking at that. Seeing the father box marked as unknown."

Robbie turned back toward the portrait. "Lorielle really didn't know, or she didn't want to acknowledge him?"

"I don't think she knew," he said, his voice rough

with emotion. "She was already living on the streets when she got pregnant."

"This is her, right?" Robbie tilted the black-framed picture toward him. "She has to be Holly's mother. They look so much alike. She doesn't even look much older than Holly."

"She wasn't. She was young, like you must have been when you got pregnant. She was about the age that Skylar is now."

"Skylar? Was she the girl with Holly?"

He nodded.

"How's she about the kiss? She seemed pretty upset." She'd seemed jealous.

"No, she was fine."

Robbie smiled at his male oblivion. "No, most likely she's not. She has a huge crush on you. And your kissing me broke her heart."

He laughed. "You're exaggerating."

"You need to be more careful," she advised.

"I put in metal detectors and hired more security guards," he reminded her. "What else do I need to do?"

"Be careful," she repeated. "You're too involved, too emotional, because of your sister. You've lost your objectivity."

He expelled a sigh of profound resignation. "I thought it might be different this visit, that you might finally approve of what I'm doing here."

"I approve," she insisted. "I'm just concerned that that girl has mistaken your love for the shelter and your sister as love for her. And she's going to get hurt. You might get hurt, too."

He shook his head in disappointment. "You've

proved to me that you're right. You can't help these kids. You won't let yourself care about anyone but Kayla. You won't let yourself get involved at all."

She drew a calming breath as her own anger flared. "I'm not going to fight with you. I realize that I struck a nerve talking about your sister and that you're lashing out at me. I understand."

He shook his head as if he pitied her. "No. You don't. You don't understand yourself. I doubt you can understand me."

He was the one who didn't understand and couldn't accept her. Robbie had been a fool to think another visit to the shelter would have done anything but prove to Holden that Robbie was *not* the woman for him.

Chapter Fifteen

Holden pivoted in his seat as much as the belt would allow, so he could glance through the Plexiglas at Jaws. The German shepherd's mouth hung open, as if he was grinning, perfectly content in the harness that strapped him to the back seat so he wouldn't be hurt if the car was involved in an accident. "Where do the criminals ride? Not back there with him?"

Ethan chuckled. "Maybe they should. Jaws would keep them in line. But I call for backup if I arrest someone. Usually *we're* the ones called out as backup to track down suspects, and the arrest belongs to someone else, anyway."

"Do you mind giving up the arrest?"

Ethan chuckled. "Nah, I don't have to handle the booking or process as much paperwork."

Holden sighed. "I hear you on the paperwork. I never thought there'd be so much involved with running a shelter."

"The CPA session you and Rafe Sanchez did about community service was real cool," Ethan praised him.

They'd taken a class field trip, meeting first at Rafe's

after-school youth center and then at the shelter. "Yeah, it was cool," he agreed. It would have been cooler had Robbie attended, but he couldn't blame her for skipping the CPA since he'd been such a jerk that day in his office.

"It was real inspiring, too," Ethan continued as he shot a sympathetic glance at Holden. "Especially the part about your sister. I'm sorry about what happened to her."

"Yeah, me, too." But maybe Robbie was right. Maybe it was time he let go of some of the guilt.

"I'm sure you and Rafe got some more volunteers to sign up for your programs. Maybe you can find someone to handle the paperwork for you."

He could have hired someone to handle the paperwork and some of the counseling, too. Maybe he had taken on too much by himself. As penance for not being there for Lorielle when she'd needed him most?

"You look like you could use more help," Ethan remarked.

"What do you mean?"

"You look dead on your feet, Rev," Ethan admonished him. "You're working too hard."

He wasn't sleeping, because every time he closed his eyes he saw Robbie's face. He missed her, and he doubted he'd see her anytime soon. In addition to not being at the CPA classes, she wasn't available for the ride-along. When he'd talked to Lieutenant O'Donnell about it, he was informed that he'd have to do a ride-along with Ethan, that Robbie had already done one.

Truth was, she wasn't available to *him*. He couldn't blame her. He'd overreacted to her observations at the shelter. She'd touched a nerve, and he'd lashed out like one of the resentful teenagers he wanted to help.

"I tried to get Robbie to come work at the shelter," he admitted.

Ethan snorted. "When would she have time? Any minute she's not working she's with her daughter. She doesn't have a minute to spare, Rev."

"I didn't want her just to volunteer in her free time. I wanted her to quit the department and work with me," he explained.

Ethan laughed so loudly Jaws barked in reaction, as if joining in. "So how hard did she hit you?"

"Why would she hit me?"

"Asking a cop to quit the job? God, Rev, that's like asking one of us to cut off a leg. We'd never be the same again. The job is part of us. For some, it's *all* of us."

"It can't be all of Robbie. She has to think about Kayla," Holden said. "She has to make sure she'll be there for her daughter."

"She will be," Ethan assured him. "She's a smart cop. She doesn't take risks."

"I was there when she chased that drug dealer on her own."

"Okay, that might not have been her smartest move. But she handled him all by herself, in the end. She's tough and prepared. She'll be fine."

"You think so?"

The sergeant nodded. "Oh, yeah. And Lakewood's not that dangerous of a city, anyhow."

"I'm not so sure about that, not after some of the things I've witnessed," Holden said.

"Sure, bad things happen here," Ethan responded. "But bad things happen everywhere—even in small towns."

"True."

"And it's looking like the chief and the mayor might be coming to an agreement about the budget. When we get more officers on the streets, it'll be safer for everyone."

Holden breathed a ragged sigh of relief.

Ethan shook his head. "I thought you and the social worker had something going on, but you have feelings for Robbie."

"Is it that obvious?"

"Officers are trained to be observant. But I think a blind man could see how you looked at her at the Lighthouse. And it killed you that she left with Sean O'Donnell."

Holden pushed a hand through his hair. "Yeah, I have it bad."

"So what are you going to do about it?"

"Nothing," Holden said. "We've both decided it would never work."

"Well, at least you agreed on something. You have that in common."

"We probably have too much in common." They were both so stubborn and single-minded.

Ethan sighed. "That'd be easier than being too different. I understand that whole 'opposites attract' thing, but I doubt they manage to stay together long when they have nothing in common."

Holden said, "I think a relationship works better when you complete each other, when you can provide the other person with something they don't have."

Ethan rubbed a hand over his face. "I never thought about it that way."

"Have you found someone special?" Holden asked.

The sergeant sighed. "I did, but it would never work—we're just too different."

"You won't know unless you try. You have nothing to lose," Holden pointed out. Whereas he had much to lose, but maybe he had even more to gain.

"True—"

A voice came over the radio. "Shots fired, corner of Lakeshore and Oak. Officer assist. Unit's been hit…"

Holden's heart slammed against his ribs as he recognized the voice. "That's Robbie. Is she saying that someone's shooting at her?" His voice cracked. "Has she been hit?"

"The car, for sure," Ethan said as he snapped on the sirens and lights.

"Just the car? Not her?" Holden needed reassurance.

"If she'd been hit, she would have said, 'Officer down.'" Ethan's hands tightened on the wheel as he sped through Lakewood. Other sirens echoed his as all units responded.

When they pulled up at the scene, lights were flashing like a Christmas show. As per the rules of the ride-along, Holden was supposed to wait until Ethan cleared him to leave the vehicle, but he opened the door and jumped out even before the car came to a complete stop.

"Where is she?" he yelled as he shoved through the people.

Lieutenant O'Donnell caught hold of him, jerking him back with his arm around him. "She's not here."

"Where is she?"

"At the hospital."

Holden's legs shook, threatening to fold beneath him. "Oh, my God…"

"No, she's fine," O'Donnell said.

"Really?" He stared at the other man through narrowed eyes. "Then why is she at the hospital?"

"She rode in the ambulance with the suspect."

"She shot him?"

"Her. But Robbie didn't shoot her. Discharging the gun hurt the girl's hand," O'Donnell explained. "She probably broke her thumb or wrist."

"And Robbie rode in the ambulance with the person who tried to kill her," Holden said, hating himself for saying she didn't care about anyone but Kayla. God, had he known her at all?

"She doesn't think the girl was trying to kill her," O'Donnell explained, "just scare her."

"Scare her?"

"Yeah, away from you." The lieutenant gestured at Ethan. "Brew will take you to the hospital, and then you'll understand what I'm talking about."

And he would be able to assure himself that Robbie was truly all right. But even if she didn't have a scratch on her, he wasn't sure his heart would ever slow back down to normal. This girl might have meant to scare Robbie, but Holden was the one who'd been scared. Terrified, in fact, that he'd lost the woman he loved.

ROBBIE TENSED her muscles, fighting the urge to sympathize with the girl's tears of pain. "You obviously never fired a gun before."

Skylar sniffled and shook her head as an intern applied plaster to her broken wrist.

"Where'd you get the gun?" Robbie asked.

"On the street."

The cheap weapon had misfired—not that Skylar would have hit Robbie if it hadn't.

"Why did you shoot at me?" Robbie had been driving through the east district when the shots had rung out, shattering the lights on top of the police cruiser.

"Because he's mine."

"Who?" Robbie asked, even though she already knew the answer.

The girl sniffled again. "Reverend Thomas."

"He's not mine, Skylar," she said. "But he's not yours, either. He's only trying to help you."

"Because he loves me."

Robbie shook her head, and now she did sympathize with the teenager, who wasn't the only one wanting Holden's love. Some noise, or perhaps a feeling, drew her attention to the privacy curtain of Skylar's corner of the busy emergency room. Holden stood there, his face tight with worry, which turned to resignation when she met his gaze.

Whatever hope she'd once harbored that he might change his mind about her being the wrong woman for him died. In his mind, he now had irrefutable proof that marrying her would be breaking his promise to Lorielle.

She waited for him to rush in and defend Skylar, but instead, he turned and walked away—leaving her puzzled and oddly disappointed.

She turned her attention back to the girl. "He loves you," she agreed, "but like he loved his sister. He's so involved because he wants to make sure you don't wind up like she did. Dead."

Skylar flinched and dropped her surly facade. The

kid was scared, as scared as Robbie remembered being when she'd run away from home. "I'm tough," the girl insisted, but her voice quavered with fear.

"Yeah, I thought I was, too, when I was living on the streets."

Skylar snorted. "You did not."

"Yup, and to make it even harder," she shared with her, "I was pregnant."

The girl's eyes widened in shock. "You were? Really?"

"It's dangerous out there, Skylar," she warned. "I know that. Holden knows that, and he's trying to protect you. He does care about you, but he isn't in love with you."

Tears streaked down the girl's already puffy face. "Why? Because he's in love with you?"

Robbie resisted the urge to laugh and shook her head. "No." If he had been close to falling for her, he wouldn't now, not since she'd proved all his fears about her were true.

Her heart aching for her own loss and also for the girl, she slid her arm around Skylar's shaking shoulders. "It's going to be okay…"

She felt like crying, too, as she uttered the lie. It wasn't going to be okay. Not for her. She'd already fallen for Holden, and she didn't know how she was going to get over him.

HOLDEN LIFTED a hand and wiped away the beads of sweat that had formed on his forehead. He'd nearly gotten sick—with relief—because she wasn't hurt. To get himself together he'd walked away, but only for a moment. He couldn't stay away from her.

Hell, he'd never been able to stay away from her. And even though he was breaking his promise, he wasn't going to try to stay away anymore. Hearing the certainty in her voice when she told Skylar that he didn't love her, Robbie, filled him with regret.

A big hand settled on his shoulder, startling him, and he whirled around to face the chief. The man must have come from home; he wore jeans and a sweater, instead of his uniform. He guided Holden back into the waiting room. "She's good with the girl," Frank Archer commented.

Just like Holden had thought she'd be, once she let down her guard and shared her experiences.

"Yes," he agreed. He wouldn't have known what to say to Skylar himself. The way he'd been talking to the girl since she'd shown up at the shelter had obviously given her the wrong impression.

"I remember the first time I saw Roberta Meyers," the chief reminisced. "She should be proud of how far she's come and how much she's achieved."

"She should." And maybe by sharing her story with Skylar, she was beginning to believe that herself.

"Now if she could just find someone who truly appreciates her and all she's accomplished," Archer said pointedly.

"Did she tell you that I asked her to quit the department and come to work at the shelter?"

The chief shook his head. "No. Someone else mentioned it."

Sergeant Brewer.

"My wife used to worry a lot about my job, too," Frank Archer said.

"I can understand why."

"I lost her just a year ago." Sorrow and regret dimmed the chief's eyes. "To cancer."

Sympathy filled Holden. And a realization. The chief, despite his dangerous career, hadn't been the one to leave his spouse behind, heartbroken with loss. "I'm sorry."

"You're still here?" Robbie asked as she walked through the E.R. doors.

Holden nodded, unable to speak as emotion clogged his throat.

"You can go see Skylar now," she said, "before I take her and book her." She looked tense, as if she expected an argument from him.

But he wasn't ready to talk to her yet, even though she deserved his apology. He simply stared at her for a full moment, their gazes locked, before he turned and pushed through the swinging doors.

He still hadn't found his voice when he ducked around the curtain and joined Skylar. Her eyes damp with tears, she met his gaze and then quickly looked away.

"You're mad at me," she said. "I'm sorry. I was such an idiot."

"You committed a serious crime," he said. "You could have killed…" He lost his voice for another minute as it cracked with fear over what could have happened. "You could have *killed* Officer Meyers."

"You love her?"

He nodded. "Yes."

She sucked in a shaky breath, then released it in a wistful sigh. "She doesn't think you do."

"That's because I've been an idiot, and I haven't told

her." He hadn't even wanted to admit it to himself—that he'd fallen so deeply in love with her that he'd never get over her, even if she didn't return his feelings.

"You should tell her," Skylar suggested.

After he'd acted like such a fool, he doubted Robbie would be interested in his love. "I think it might be too late."

"Like it's too late for me," the teenager said with resignation. "So what's going to happen to me now?"

"Officer Meyers has to arrest you."

"I know. I mean, what do I do?"

He opened his mouth, ready to offer her a lawyer and bail money. But then she asked, "Should I call my mom, like Officer Meyers said?"

"Officer Meyers suggested that?"

"Yeah, she thinks maybe my mom got smart and ditched the loser boyfriend." Hope flickered in her eyes. "Maybe Mom wants me to come home."

And maybe Skylar wanted to go home—now that she accepted the fact that Holden wasn't in love with her. Why hadn't he noticed her feelings for him? He'd been so intent on trying to protect her that he hadn't realized he might have sent the wrong message. He didn't want to do that again. "Skylar, you're in a lot of trouble. You may not be able to go home."

"Officer Meyers said she'd talk to the district attorney and get the charges reduced," the girl said. "She thinks she can probably get me probation."

"She's going to do that after you shot at her?" he asked, awed again by the woman he loved.

"She's not what I thought she was." Skylar had been one of the teenagers who had called the vice cop names when Roberta had walked into the shelter with him. "She's pretty cool."

"Yeah, she is." If she could forgive a girl who'd shot at her, maybe she could forgive him, too, for being such a jerk.

Chapter Sixteen

Robbie blinked, trying to clear the grit from her eyes so that she could see to put her key in the lock of her apartment door. She had been awake for so many hours that her muscles trembled with exhaustion. But she wasn't just physically tired. She was emotionally worn-out, too.

When she came off a tough shift like this she longed to see her daughter's face, to hold the girl close and remind herself that it was all worth it. Kayla made all her hard work worth the effort. She needed to hold her daughter so badly right now that she even considered dropping by her school. Yet was it really that she needed to hold someone, or was it that she needed to be held?

Finally the key turned, and then she rotated the knob and opened the door by leaning against the wood. Yawning, she stumbled across the threshold. And into a pair of strong arms that caught her and held her close to a chest in which a heart pounded fast and hard.

Trembling fingers combed back her hair from her face. "Robbie…"

Her breath shuddered out with relief. "You're here."

She tipped up her chin and met his gaze, her eyes narrowed in confusion. "*How* are you here?"

"Joelly let me in."

She didn't even care that her friend had broken her promise to quit matchmaking. She closed her arms around his waist and held on tight. "Did you see Kayla?"

His chin brushed over her hair as he shook his head. "I just missed her. But Joelly said she seemed fine when she got her ready for school this morning. She said that Kayla understands that sometimes you have to work past your shift. Why did you have to work past your shift?"

"Paperwork," she said.

"Or were you talking to the district attorney on Skylar's behalf?"

"That, too," she admitted with a weary sigh. "I honestly don't think she meant to hurt me. She's just a screwed-up kid."

"I should have seen that she was getting too attached to me," he said, his voice thick with guilt and regret. "I'm the counselor. But I was too close. You were right, I lost my objectivity. I was trying so hard to save…"

"Lorielle."

"Yeah, but she's gone."

At the resignation in his voice, she tipped back her head and met his gaze. "That's not your fault," she said.

"I'm going to try to accept that now." His arms tightened around her. "And I'm going to try to be more objective."

"You'll lose your objectivity again because you care so much," she said with respect. "You were right about me, that I don't get involved enough."

"It's not because you don't care, though," he replied. "I was wrong to ever think that. You showed me, with the way you handled Skylar, that you care. I overheard some of your conversation with her and then I talked to her myself. You got through to her. You're good with teenagers."

Robbie closed her eyes on a wave of weariness. "I'm not strong enough to fight with you right now."

"I don't want to fight."

"And I don't want to quit my job," she said.

He cupped her face in his palms, his hands trembling slightly. "I don't want you to quit your job."

His admission stunned her. "I thought after last night, after the shooting, that you'd be even more adamant that I quit."

"Skylar's shooting at you had nothing to do with your job and everything to do with me," he said, his voice filled with emotion and his eyes dark with guilt and regret. "That was my fault. I put you in danger."

"It wasn't your fault. You had no idea how she felt," she told him. And she had a feeling he had no idea how she felt, how much she loved him.

"You told me," he reminded her, "and I acted like an ass about it."

"You didn't see it yourself."

"I should have," he said. "I'm going to hire more people."

"You have enough security now."

"I'm going to hire more counselors and an administrator."

"I hope you still intend to let volunteers work at the shelter," she said, "because I'd like to help out there."

She studied his face, trying to gauge his reaction, but he revealed nothing of his thoughts.

"I'd love to have you help out."

"It won't be too awkward?" she asked.

"The kids will accept you. You'll get through to them like you got through to Skylar last night."

He was the one she wanted to get through to. He'd said he didn't want her to quit her job. Was that because he'd completely given up on a future for them?

"What about you?" she asked. "Will you ever accept me?" She had to know.

"Robbie—"

"I'm not asking you to break your promise to Lorielle."

"I wouldn't."

She flinched, knowing now that he didn't feel the same way about her that she felt about him. She had made a horrible mistake, so she stepped back until his hands fell from her shoulders. "Oh…"

"I'm not breaking my promise to her," he said.

Her heart clutched, and she bit her lip so that she would not beg him to give her a chance. "We're back where we were, then. Stalemate."

Tears of hopelessness and exhaustion threatened. Too tired to fight them, Roberta simply closed her eyes to hold them in.

"Look at me," he said.

When she opened her eyes, she discovered that he had dropped to his knees in front of her. "What are you doing?"

"I'm proposing," he said, his pulse racing with adrenaline. "If you'll have me as your husband, I'd be honored if you became my bride, Roberta Meyers."

She pressed her hand to her heart, trying to slow its mad pounding. "I don't understand…"

"I love you," he vowed. "I want to spend the rest of my life with you and Kayla and Holly."

"But your promise…"

"Will be kept." He nodded his head. "Whether you stay in vice or transfer to the SRT or join the bomb unit, we'll still provide the security of a loving family that I promised my sister I would give her daughter."

"Are you serious?" she asked in a whisper.

"Very serious," he assured her. "I love you." He would keep saying it until she believed him and because, if something had happened to her, he never would have forgiven himself for not telling her. "I want to marry you so we can take care of each other and our kids. What's your answer, Robbie?"

"Yes, yes!" She threw her arms around his neck.

Clasping her in his arms, he rose from his knees. Then he carried her down the hall to the bedroom. Sunlight streamed through the blinds and bathed her face as he laid her on the bed.

She tugged him down and kissed him. "I love you, too. I love you so much, Holden Thomas. I can't wait to become your bride."

"We'll marry right away," he promised. "As soon as we can get a marriage license."

Her fingers fumbled with buttons as she opened his shirt. "Get undressed," she ordered him.

"Robbie, you're so tired you could barely get the key in the lock," he reminded her, his heart aching with concern and love for her. "Why don't you go to sleep? I'll just hold you."

"I'm not tired anymore." Her blue eyes sparkled with excitement and anticipation. "I'll never be too tired to make love with you."

"Can we make that part of our wedding vows?" he teased.

Her breath audibly caught. "You really asked me to marry you?"

"Yes, I really did. And you said yes." He smiled. "So don't change your mind now."

She shook her head. "Never."

"I was so scared tonight," he admitted as he cupped her face in his palms. "When I heard you on the radio, I was terrified I would lose you. And I hadn't told you I loved you. I wouldn't have been able to live with myself if something had happened to you."

"Nothing happened," she spoke gently, reassuringly. "I'm fine."

"You're perfect," he said and kissed her.

Her lips clung to his while she skimmed her hands up his chest. "You're the perfect one," she murmured into his mouth.

He grinned. "How about we're both perfect—for each other?"

"Yes," she agreed. "Now make love to your fiancée."

"I'd love to."

Undressing her slowly, he kissed every inch of silky skin he exposed. He lavished extra attention on her beautiful breasts, teasing her nipples into tight points with his tongue. Then he slid lower and made love to her with his mouth until she arched away from the bed and cried out.

"Holden!"

He tore off his shirt and scrambled out of his shoes, jeans and boxers. In seconds he buried himself deep inside her wet heat. She locked her legs around his waist, meeting each of his thrusts in perfect harmony. And in perfect harmony, they came.

Pleasure tore through him, shattering his control. Panting for breath, he collapsed in her arms, then rolled to his side with her locked against him. He was filled with a peace he'd never known. He closed his eyes and murmured, "Robbie…"

She gently slapped his cheek with her palm. "Don't fall asleep," she ordered him.

Holden groaned. "You're not going to kick me out of bed again, are you?"

"Yes," she said with a girlish giggle of pure happiness.

His heart swelled with joy that he had made her that happy, as happy as she made him.

"I'm going to kick us both out," she said. "We need to go someplace."

"But we were both awake all night. Can't we just close our eyes for a while?" he negotiated.

"What we have to do is more important than sleeping," she promised.

A grin spread across his lips as he realized where she wanted to go. "Of course. It is much more important."

"My mom never came home last night," Kayla whispered to Holly.

Holly leaned her fair head against Kayla's temple. "Do you think she was with my uncle?" she asked.

"Did you see her at your house?"

"No," Holly replied. "But he wasn't home, either. I

just figured he had to go to the shelter. But maybe they were together."

"Aunt JoJo said Mom had to work late."

"Did she say why?" Holly asked. Her voice got all high, as if she was scared, too.

"No."

"Does she do that much?"

"She's usually not this late." Kayla wrapped an arm around her stomach. It had begun to hurt. "She usually gets me ready for school in the morning—no matter how late she works."

"That's cool," Holly said, blinking like she was trying not to cry.

"You must miss your mom a lot," Kayla said, and under the table where they sat together in class, she slid her hand into Holly's.

Holly squeezed her fingers. "It's not that. She wasn't that kind of mom. She was gone a lot, but she'd leave me with Uncle Holden. So I was okay with it. I wasn't surprised when she didn't come back the last time." Tears shimmered in her eyes. "I was actually happy she didn't come back. Does that make me horrible?"

"No," Kayla told her friend. "Your uncle is great. You wanted to stay with him. Your mom… She wasn't a good mom."

"Not like your mom," Holly said. "I hope she comes home."

Kayla blinked. "I'm sure she will. She always comes home. She's a lot tougher than the bad guys."

"Hey, look!" Holly whispered, pointing to the door where her uncle's head was visible through the window.

Kayla closed her eyes, scared he'd come down to

give her bad news about her mom. She heard the door open and squeezed Holly's hand tighter.

"Look!" Holly urged her, her voice shaking with excitement.

Kayla sucked in a deep breath and opened her eyes. Then she blinked because she didn't believe what she saw. Mom and Uncle Holden walked in the door, hand in hand, like her and Holly. "What's going on?" she asked her friend.

"I don't know, but your mom's okay."

"Yeah, she is." And she had the biggest smile on her face Kayla had ever seen.

"We have something to tell you two," Mom said. "Let's go out in the hall."

"Oh!" Holly shouted as she did when she got the answer to a question before everyone else. "I know— you two are getting married!"

Her uncle Holden laughed. "There's no fooling you, honey."

"Really?" Kayla asked, staring up at her mom. "You're getting married?"

"How do you feel about that?"

Kayla turned to Holly, and they both jumped up and screamed, "We're sisters!"

"We're really sisters," Holly said.

"We're a family," Uncle Holden said.

Tears poured from Kayla's eyes as she realized it was true. They were a family. She now had a mom, a dad and a sister. Her mom pulled her into her arms.

"Are you okay, sweetheart?" she asked as she wiped the tears from Kayla's face. "What's wrong?"

"N-nothing," she said. Everything was so right.

"Then why are you crying so hard?"

"Because I've never been so happy."

"Me, neither," her mom said as she glanced up at Holden and then over at Holly and smiled. "I have never been so happy."

And then the four of them huddled together in what Kayla knew would be the first of many, many group hugs. Her life was now perfect.

Silhouette® Romantic SUSPENSE

**Sparked by Danger,
Fueled by Passion.**

The Agent's Secret Baby

by *USA TODAY* bestselling author

Marie Ferrarella

**TOP SECRET
DELIVERIES**

Dr. Eve Walters suddenly finds herself pregnant
after a regrettable one-night stand and turns to an
online chat room for support. She eventually learns
the true identity of her one-night stand: a DEA agent
with a deadly secret. Adam Serrano does not want
this baby or a relationship, but can fear for Eve's
and the baby's lives convince him that this is what
he has been searching for after all?

Available October wherever books are sold.

**Look for upcoming titles in
the TOP SECRET DELIVERIES miniseries**

The Cowboy's Secret Twins by Carla Cassidy—November
The Soldier's Secret Daughter by Cindy Dees—December

Visit Silhouette Books at www.eHarlequin.com

In 2009 Harlequin celebrates
60 years of pure reading pleasure!

We're marking this occasion by offering
16 **FREE** full books to download and read.

Visit

www.HarlequinCelebrates.com

to choose from a variety of
great romance stories
that are absolutely **FREE!**

(Total approximate retail value of $60)

We invite you to visit and share the Web site
with your friends, family
and anyone who enjoys reading.

You're invited to join our Tell Harlequin Reader Panel!

By joining our new reader panel you will:

- Receive Harlequin® books—they are FREE and yours to keep with no obligation to purchase anything!
- Participate in fun online surveys
- Exchange opinions and ideas with women just like you
- Have a say in our new book ideas and help us publish the best in women's fiction

In addition, you will have a chance to win great prizes and receive special gifts! See Web site for details. Some conditions apply. Space is limited.

To join, visit us at
www.TellHarlequin.com.

#1 *New York Times*
bestselling author

DEBBIE MACOMBER

Dear Reader,

I'm not much of a letter writer. As the sheriff here, I'm used to writing incident reports, not chatty letters. But my daughter, Megan—who'll be making me a grandfather soon—told me I had to do this. So here goes.

I'll tell you straight out that I'd hoped to marry Faith Beckwith (my onetime high school girlfriend) but she ended the relationship last month, even though we're both widowed and available.

However, I've got plenty to keep me occupied, like the unidentified remains found in a cave outside town. And the fact that my friend Judge Olivia Griffin is fighting cancer. And the break-ins at 204 Rosewood Lane—the house Faith happens to be renting from Grace Harding...

If you want to hear more, come on over to my place or to the sheriff's office (if you can stand the stale coffee!).

Troy Davis

92 Pacific Boulevard

Available August 25
wherever books are sold!

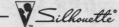

SPECIAL EDITION

FROM *NEW YORK TIMES*
BESTSELLING AUTHOR

SUSAN MALLERY

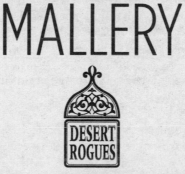

DESERT ROGUES

THE SHEIK AND THE BOUGHT BRIDE

Victoria McCallan works in Prince Kateb's palace.
When Victoria's gambling father is caught cheating
at cards with the prince, Victoria saves her father from
going to jail by being Kateb's mistress for six months.
But the darkly handsome desert sheik isn't as harsh as
Victoria thinks he is, and Kateb finds himself attracted to
his new mistress. But Kateb has already loved and lost
once—is he willing to give love another try?

Available in October wherever books are sold.

SSE65481

REQUEST YOUR FREE BOOKS!

2 FREE NOVELS PLUS 2 FREE GIFTS!

◆ HARLEQUIN®

American ★ Romance®

Love, Home & Happiness!

YES! Please send me 2 FREE Harlequin® American Romance® novels and my 2 FREE gifts (gifts are worth about $10). After receiving them, if I don't wish to receive any more books, I can return the shipping statement marked "cancel." If I don't cancel, I will receive 4 brand-new novels every month and be billed just $4.24 per book in the U.S. or $4.99 per book in Canada.* That's a savings of close to 15% off the cover price! It's quite a bargain! Shipping and handling is just 50¢ per book. I understand that accepting the 2 free books and gifts places me under no obligation to buy anything. I can always return a shipment and cancel at any time. Even if I never buy another book from Harlequin, the two free books and gifts are mine to keep forever.

154 HDN E4DS   354 HDN E4D4

Name	(PLEASE PRINT)	
Address		Apt. #
City	State/Prov.	Zip/Postal Code

Signature (if under 18, a parent or guardian must sign)

Mail to the **Harlequin Reader Service:**
IN U.S.A.: P.O. Box 1867, Buffalo, NY 14240-1867
IN CANADA: P.O. Box 609, Fort Erie, Ontario L2A 5X3

Not valid to current subscribers of Harlequin® American Romance® books.

Want to try two free books from another line?
Call 1-800-873-8635 or visit www.morefreebooks.com.

* Terms and prices subject to change without notice. Prices do not include applicable taxes. N.Y. residents add applicable sales tax. Canadian residents will be charged applicable provincial taxes and GST. Offer not valid in Quebec. This offer is limited to one order per household. All orders subject to approval. Credit or debit balances in a customer's account(s) may be offset by any other outstanding balance owed by or to the customer. Please allow 4 to 6 weeks for delivery. Offer available while quantities last.

Your Privacy: Harlequin is committed to protecting your privacy. Our Privacy Policy is available online at www.eHarlequin.com or upon request from the Reader Service. From time to time we make our lists of customers available to reputable third parties who may have a product or service of interest to you. If you would prefer we not share your name and address, please check here. ☐

HAR09R2

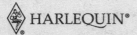

HARLEQUIN®

American ★ Romance®

COMING NEXT MONTH
Available October 13, 2009

#1277 TOP GUN DAD by Ann DeFee
Men Made in America
Flying missions for the U.S. Air Force seems easy compared to being a single father. Between dealing with teenage angst and starting a new life in Oklahoma, pilot Chad Cassavetes has no time for romance. But then he meets Kelbie Montgomery, an intriguing single mom who has sworn off military men. Can Chad change Kelbie's rules of engagement—and become her very own top gun?

#1278 A BABY FOR MOMMY by Cathy Gillen Thacker
The Lone Star Dads Club
Mealtimes were mayhem before busy single father Dan Kingsland took on a personal chef. Too bad that when he hired the wonderful Emily Stayton he didn't notice the baby bump under her coat. Now the single mother-to-be is leaving Fort Worth after Thanksgiving…unless Dan can convince Emily that her baby needs a dad, as much as his kids need a mother.

#1279 MISTLETOE HERO by Tanya Michaels
4 Seasons in Mistletoe
Arianne Waide has always felt an important part of her small-town Georgia community. She wants Gabe Sloan to feel that way, too—which is why she's making the resident bad boy her personal mission. But old rumors still follow Gabe, keeping him an outsider in his own town. Until, that is, he has a chance to show everyone what it takes to be a *real* hero.

#1280 THE LITTLEST MATCHMAKER by Dorien Kelly
The last thing busy bakery owner and single mother Lisa Kincaid needs is to start dating again. So why is the Iowa widow starting to look at sexy construction-company owner Kevin Decker in a new light? Their friendship is about to blossom into something new and exciting—with a little push from a four-year-old Cupid!

www.eHarlequin.com